Night Express

I walk with my candle held high, checking the slim platoons of silent, empty seats. My spirits would be raised if I could only spy a sandwich box or a sports bag, a woolly scarf or a magazine – some sign that we might not be the only people left alive.

All the tables and seats are empty.

'What's happened to everyone?'

But Marie is staring ahead at the window that looks through the next set of doors.

'What's the matter?'

'Can you see that?'

'What?'

'Just behind the door. Look.'

We both pause.

Behind the window at the end of the carriage is a large, dark shadow. We both stand still for a moment. 'Do you think it's. . .?'

Linda Hoy

Nightmare Express

Collins

An imprint of HarperCollinsPublishers

First published in Great Britain by Collins in 1996
Collins in an imprint of HarperCollins*Publishers* Ltd.,
77 - 85 Fulham Palace Road, Hammersmith,
London W6 8JB

1 3 5 7 9 8 6 4 2

Copyright © Linda Hoy 1996

ISBN 0 00 674926 7

The author asserts the moral right to be identified
as the author of the work.

Printed and bound in Great Britain
by HarperCollins Manufacturing Ltd., Glasgow.

Nightmare Express is dedicated to the Lescar's Gelati quiz team - to Leo, Mick and Jane, Patrick, Pedro, Pete, Simon and of course, our inspirational team leader, John Sanella.

1

'Ta-da-da-daaa!'

'Surprise! Surprise!'

Our train's just pulling out of Sheffield station as Marie opens up her rucksack and pulls out a glossy brochure. 'Just as I promised, Teresa, I've brought something very special for you.'

'Well then, let's have a look.'

Marie places the brochure on top of our pile of sandwiches. On its cover leers a grimacing skull and – in dripping red –

THE YORK DUNGEON

'You and I, my dear,' Marie gloats, tapping her finger between the skull's gaping eye sockets, 'are going somewhere *very special*.'

'Where?'

'Here. Have a look.'

I open up the brochure with excitement but, as I turn the pages, I'm confronted with the most gruesome scenes of blood, torture and mutilation. 'Ugh!'

Marie bites into her paté sandwich. 'Good, isn't it?'

A broken-necked body dangles from a hangman's noose; men are burned, branded and beheaded. I flick through the pages to encounter even more dismembered bodies, blood and entrails. 'It's disgusting!'

'I know,' Marie splutters through her paté.

'It's revolting!'

'Look at this one; *Margaret Clitherow*.' Marie points

to the blood-soaked body jutting from underneath a wooden board on which a ghoulish ruffian is piling heavy rocks. She rests her finger on one of the stones. 'We can build this up into our project.'

I chuckle and shake my head. 'When Sister told us about the martyrdom of Margaret Clitherow, she never said anything about . . .' I glance at the picture and shudder, 'about her battered body with ribs bursting through its skin. Sister would have a heart attack if she thought we were going somewhere full of these . . . well, full of . . .'

Marie wags her finger, imitating Sister Frances in Morning Assembly: 'Lost souls,' she croaks. 'Those who have lost their way. Those who live lives of fantasy and nightmare . . .

'This is what happens,' she warns, pointing to the various unspeakable instruments of torture, 'to girls who drop litter in the school corridor.' She indicates a hapless victim being roasted in a cauldron over an open fire. 'This is what happens to those pupils who do not wear their full school uniform.' She points her finger accusingly at my big woolly jumper.

I giggle.

Both of us, of course, are wearing our normal clothes for our day out in York, in spite of the rule that school uniform must always be worn on every possible occasion.

Marie opens her can of Coke, spraying me with fizz. 'And now, children,' she chuckles, 'time for this morning's hymn . . .'

I glance outside at the green dome of Meadowhall shopping centre and the vast car parks. It's the first time we've been on a train on our own and I can't help feeling excited. Especially as the rest of our class will just be filing into Assembly.

6

'Come on. Sing out everyone!'

Marie clears a space in between the sandwiches and raises both her hands to impersonate Sister Frances poised at her piano:

> *I'm on the right track with Jesus . . .*

she starts off.

I start to giggle.

> *I'm on the right lines with the Lord –*

I glance around the carriage. There's no one sitting near us, so we both start chortling together:

> *He will take me by the hand*
> *And lead me to the promised land –*

we chorus:

> *Oh yes, I'm on the right track with the Lord.*

*

'Well,' pronounced Dr Pattram, straightening her sari across her shoulder, 'we've certainly got on the wrong tracks here. We've made a very bad mistake in allowing Donald too much freedom.'

Carter pressed his lips together.

'This patient is much too dangerous to be on an open ward. We cannot take the risk of him wandering round the grounds and disturbing other patients.'

Carter took a long, deep breath. But we can't punish him Dr Pattram. 'I mean, he hasn't done anything wrong. The incident with the trolley was an accident.'

Su Pattram slapped the overflowing folder of notes down on her desk. 'And what about the electric wheel-chair? What about the runaway lawn mower that scraped Myrtle Springs's bumper in the car park?' She tightened her grip on the folder. 'And what about the wheelie bin?'

Carter had to cover his face with his hand as he re-

7

membered the powder blue Toyota Supra after its encounter in the car park.

Myrtle Springs, chair of the hospital management board, was just closing her car door when the wheelie bin, loaded with potato peelings, waste food, soiled paper plates and napkins, bumped down the hill towards her.

'The runaway train came down the hill and she blew, whooo . . .'

Donald Valley panted along behind it, a tiny train driver's cap perched on top of his head.

Myrtle might have tried to stop the wheelie bin if its lid had not been open. However, the pile of potato peelings and squashed tomatoes caused her to step aside.

'The runaway train came down the hill and she blew, whooo . . . ,' sang Donald.

Towards the bottom of the bank was a STAFF PARK-ING sign. The bin teetered against it before tipping over and spilling its entire contents across the bonnet of Myrtle's spotless, shining car.

Don puffed along a few seconds behind, waving a table tennis bat and blowing on a silver whistle. 'We apologise for the sudden arrival of this train.'

Myrtle gaped in horror at the left-over hospital dinners smeared across her smoke-grey laminated windscreen and the dollops of tomato ketchup splattered across her head-lights.

Carter remembered the song the kitchen staff had composed about the wheelie bin to sing at the staff Christmas party:

> *My air conditioning's all bunged up with gravy*
> *My electric windows won't whirr up and down;*
> *My windscreen wiper's bent*
> *and I want to know who sent*

the wheelie bin that tumbled upside down . . .
Yes, the wheelie bin that tumbled upside down.

Carter managed to compose himself as Sumitra removed Don's Thomas the Tank Engine scrapbook from the cardboard box on her desk. 'Look at this . . .'

HEADLESS BODY FOUND ON RAILWAY LINE

'. . . It was Don who reported this incident to the police.'
    Carter was silent.
    'And look at this . . .

TRAGEDY AT LEVEL CROSSING

'. . . Don had some involvement here as well. He was certainly in the area.' Su Pattram turned over the pages of neatly-pasted press cuttings. 'Don isn't just obsessed with trains, Nurse Knowle, you see. He's obsessed with accidents, with carnage.

SCHOOLBOYS DIE IN TRAIN INFERNO

'He was the first to arrive on the scene at this accident and phone the newspapers with all the details. Can you think why that might be?'
    Carter shook his head in disbelief. 'You can't imagine he was responsible for . . . ?'
    Su flicked across the pages. 'This is not some harmless, childish hobby.'

RAIL TRAGEDY LEAVES SIX DEAD

She rested her forefinger on the photograph of two trains teetering up a grassy bank, their carriages mangled together. 'This man is obsessed with chaos and destruction.

INFERNO AT KING'S CROSS

'The police have already expressed the greatest possible concern.'

Carter took a deep breath. 'But, Dr Pattram, they haven't found any evidence that Don's been responsible. I mean, a man's innocent until he's been proved guilty.'

There was a pause. 'Or,' replied Su Pattram softly, 'until he's been found to be insane . . .'

2

'Well,' says Marie, biting into her first sausage roll, 'at least we've been saved from Sister's driving.'

The driving of Sister Frances is legendary in our school. The bottle bank – situated in a corner of the yard where Sister does her six-point turns with the school minibus – is now dented on all sides. It used to be circular and is now a battered octagon. The SLOW, CHILDREN CROSSING sign on the main road teeters drunkenly from its various encounters with Sister's left-hand turns; and the lollipop lady leaps for cover whenever she hears the nunmobile screeching down the drive.

'It was a near thing, though . . .'

It's three weeks now since that awesome morning when Marie and I sat side by side on the straight-backed wooden chairs in front of Sister's desk.

'So you're asking permission to take a day off school?'

I remember staring down at my feet, unable to see how we could possibly get away with Marie's amazing plan to spend a whole day skiving on our own.

'We will be working, though, Sister,' Marie insisted. 'We'll be going to York to do our research on Margaret Clitherow.'

'Mmm.' Sister stared at her private altar with its white embroidered cloth, silver crucifix and candlesticks. 'And exactly how do you intend to spend your day in York?'

That had already been decided. 'We'll go round all the shops,' Marie had insisted, 'we'll seek out some seriously scrumptious cafés and pig out on sticky buns. We'll go to the automata museum where they've got all these robots and things . . .'

Marie had gazed piously at her feet. 'Apparently, Sister, we can actually visit the blessed saint's private chapel in the Shambles.'

Sister nodded.

'We heard it would be open for private meditation.'

Marie held out her hand towards mine underneath the chair seats. She had her fingers crossed.

'That's correct.'

'We thought we could do some research in the library, and visit the Bar Convent . . .'

I crossed my fingers as well as we linked hands and stared reverently at the altar. Neither of us dared look at Sister's face, inspecting us with eyes like radar dishes, the long black hairs growing out of her warts quivering like rats' whiskers. 'Well,' she mused, 'it could be a useful opportunity for you to ask questions about . . . well, you may, for example, consider who was responsible for Margaret's death.'

Sister looked questioningly at me. 'Why do you think she died, Teresa?'

Needless to say, I'd got no idea. 'Erm . . . because she was a martyr . . . ?'

'Mmm.' Sister didn't seem too sure. 'Well. Perhaps that's the question you can ask yourselves: Who exactly was responsible?'

Marie and I both nodded enthusiastically.

'Of course, you'll both be going in your school uniforms and returning straight back afterwards.'

But Marie had everything worked out. 'Well, actually, Sister, we were hoping to visit York Minster as well. Apparently they've got a wonderful bookshop. Teresa and I were hoping to buy some . . .' she faltered momentarily.

'Prayer guides,' I mumbled.

'That's right. Prayer guides and . . . well . . .'

'. . . inspirational posters,' I offered.

Sister took out her diary. 'Well, if you're thinking of travelling on a Wednesday – that's the day I visit Agnes in St Aiden's. The hospital's near York. I could perhaps make a detour . . .'

Marie and I both shook our heads in horror. 'Oh no, we wouldn't want to put you to any trouble, Sister,' Marie insisted. 'Teresa and I were planning to go to York by train.'

'Do you think your parents will give you both permission to travel by train on your own?'

Both of us nodded. We were actually thinking of telling them it was a compulsory part of our school syllabus.

Sister gazed at her altar. 'It's a pity you can't come with me to St Aiden's, girls,' she told us sadly.

I shot Marie a sideways glance.

'I've seen the most tragic cases in that hospital. It makes one realize, you see, just how fortunate we are to be of sound mind . . .'

Marie raised her hand to her mouth, spluttered and coughed.

'Do you know, girls,' Sister shook her head in disbelief, 'I've even seen one young man in that psychiatric hospital who appears to believe that he's a train?'

*

Choo-choo-choo; choo-choo-choo . . .

> *Down by the station, early in the morning,*
> *See the little puffer-trains, all in a row . . .*

Don pistoned his large hairy arms backwards and forwards as he chugged along the corridor.

> *See the little driver blow his little whistle . . .*

13

Carter knocked on the door of Dr Pattram's office while Don let out a long hiss of steam:

Chhh-h-h-h . . .

'Come in.'

Off we go!

Carter opened the door.

With another spurt of steam, Don spluttered forward into the office, fists clenched and elbows chugging. 'We apologise for the late arrival of this train . . .'

'Good morning, Donald.'

Carter smiled politely at Dr Pattram as he closed the door behind Don.

'. . . this was due to a signal failure and problems with leaves on the line.'

'Do sit down.'

Don pulled up the collar of his train driver's jacket. He scrutinised authoritatively the empty chair in front of Sumitra's desk. 'Is this a station?'

Su raised her eyebrows and said nothing. After Don had continued to chug in circles round the room for a few seconds, she reluctantly nodded her head. 'Yes, Don, you're at a station now. You can sit down.'

'This train terminates here,' Don sank his huge weight into the plastic chair. 'All change.'

Su pulled her sari straight across her knees and pulled her mouth into the resemblance of a smile. 'Well, Donald,' she said, averting her eyes from his huge backside overhanging the edges of the chair, 'How have we been this week?'

Chooo-ooo-ooo.

'You do remember me, don't you?'

Don looked curiously at her.

Sumitra leant forward. 'I am a *doctor*, Donald. Can you remember what that means?'

14

'Please remember to take all your belongings with you.'

Sumitra tried not to stare at the line of dark tattoos, strung like a necklace round Don's flabby neck. 'A doctor is someone who makes people better.'

'And please do not open the doors until the train has reached a standstill.'

Su sighed deeply before she began again. 'Sometimes, Don, people break down. Sometimes they . . .' she searched for a word that Don would understand '. . . they crash. Like trains sometimes crash. Doctors are people who help them pick up the pieces. They help put people back together. Doctors make people well.'

Don grinned.

'Anyway, Donald, I've asked you to come and see me this morning to discuss something very important.'

Don removed a small plastic train from his pocket. He gave it a little test run up and down the back of his hand.

'There's been considerable damage done to vehicles in the staff car park. I have a feeling you might be able to tell us more about it . . .'

3

By the time our train has left Rotherham, we've eaten most of the picnic. Our table is littered with empty crisp bags, Coke cans, sandwich wrappers and crumbs.

'Well,' insists Marie, stuffing the debris into a plastic bag, 'we didn't want to be carrying that lot round with us all day, did we?'

I personally would have saved our picnic until we were really hungry, but Marie doesn't believe in saving things.

'And we need to work up an appetite for all the caffs and sticky bun shops later on.'

I glance down at the pictures in the Dungeon brochure – the blood-splattered bodies, the burning flesh and severed limbs. 'We might not feel like lots of cakes and stuff after we've been to the Dungeon.'

'Yes we will.' Marie slides the rubbish bag underneath our table and takes out her map of York.

'One thing we've got to do,' I remind her, 'is decide what our project's going to be. I mean, what are we going to do about Margaret Clitherow? Just write about her?'

Marie pulls a face. 'That'd be boring.' She stares through the window as we trundle past the backs of factories and houses, garden sheds and greenhouses, rows of cabbages and clusters of pigeon lofts. 'We could make a model of that relic Sister Frances told us about.'

I grin. 'You mean the four-hundred-year-old severed hand?'

Marie's face lights up. 'We could make it out of papier-mâché.'

'Have you remembered the candle?'

16

She nods. 'And the three matches.'

Sister Frances explained to us about the severed hand
while we were scoffing our sausages and chips. We were
sitting in the school dining hall with Bernadette
Dronfield – trying to put her off her diet by waving
chips in front of her face – when Marie started singing,
'Da-da-da-da. Da-da-da-da . . . Batwoman.'

'Where? Flying this way?'

'Think so,' Marie hissed. 'Look holy.'

We composed our faces, Marie and I gazing reverently down at our platefuls of chips and Bernadette
poring piously over her crispbread with low-fat spread
and letttuce. From the corner of my eye I glimpsed the
long black habit glide towards our table. 'She'd better
not say we can't go to York.'

Marie and myself both pressed our palms discreetly
together. 'Please, Holy Virgin . . . please let us go to
York.'

'Perhaps it'll just be a lecture on Not Talking to
Strange Men,' suggested Bernadette.

'Or Being Careful Crossing the Roads,' said Marie.

'Good morning, girls.'

'Good morning, Sister.'

'Everything ready for Wednesday?'

'Yes, thank you, Sister.'

'Well, we've got interviews at school on Wednesday
morning,' Sister explained, 'so I'm afraid you'll have to
go on your own, after all.'

'That's quite all right, Sister,' I spluttered through
my chips. 'We've already bought our tickets for the
train.'

'Well, I've brought you a map of York.' Sister
reached inside her cavernous briefcase.

'Thank you very much, Sister.'

17

'Now, girls, if you are going on the train, I must warn you to be very careful. Watch out for . . . well, there can be some quite unsavoury characters about nowadays. Don't talk to any strange men.'

I struggled to keep a straight face as I speared my sausage with my fork.

'And the roads in York can be very busy. There are some pedestrian precincts but you still need to be very careful of the traffic.'

Marie raised her eyebrows towards the ceiling. I focused my attention on Bernadette's slice of crispbread. Bernadette has been on a diet ever since we've known her. She now has a perfectly normal figure but her aim is to look like a spaghetti jar.

'And I want to ask you a favour . . .' Sister's long, black sleeves fluttered back inside her briefcase. 'I'd like you to light a candle . . . for Agnes.'

All of us widened our eyes in disbelief; my sausage paused partway to my open mouth.

'I know you'll be calling at the Convent of the Bar. There are some beautiful paintings and stained-glass windows in the chapel there; you'll want to see those. And before you leave, I'm sure the Sisters will allow you to light this candle.'

None of us said anything.

'Did you know that the Sisters have a relic of the Blessed Saint Margaret?'

Marie and I both shook our heads.

'I can tell Sister Gregory to expect you.' Sister said this as though it was an extra-special treat, 'and I'll ask her if she'll allow you to see the relic.'

Marie appeared to be choking slightly. 'What . . . what exactly is the, er . . . the relic?'

Sister clasped her hands and gazed piously at our

18

platefuls of sausages and chips. 'It's a relic,' she explained, 'of Blessed Margaret's hand.'

There was a pause.

'Just one?' Marie asked.

Sister nodded.

'But it must be . . . well, four hundred years old.'

Sister nodded again.

'How exactly did it . . . I mean, how did it well, get separated from the . . . from the rest of her?' Marie's eyes began to light up with the prospect of adding a four-hundred-year-old grisly relic to our itinerary.

I just replaced my forked sausage back on to my plate.

'The priest who took Margaret's last confession – he was involved with the Convent. I think he was the one that . . .'

There was another pause. Marie and I were both waiting for Sister to add *sawed her hand off* but, for once, Sister Frances seemed lost for words.

'So, whilst you're there, if you'd be kind enough to light this.' Sister produced a small white candle from her briefcase. She then counted out three matches and slid them into an empty box which she passed to Marie.

Marie stood the candle on our formica-topped table between the salt and pepper and the vinegar.

'I've been very concerned about poor Agnes,' Sister explained. 'I do fear that she's beginning to lose her grip on reality.'

Marie glanced swiftly at me with eyebrows raised. We once had a close encounter with Poor Agnes, a schoolteacher who turned into a witch. After accounting for the disappearance of several unsuspecting teenagers, she almost skewered Marie and myself in a gingerbread cottage with a sharpened broomstick. In fact we might have been roasted alive if . . . well, we told that story in

Nightmare Park but we did decide there and then that Agnes was two wafers short of an ice-cream sandwich.

'So, if you'd be kind enough, girls, to light this candle before you leave the chapel, then say a short prayer for the poor lost souls in St Aiden's and the caring doctors and nurses who devote their lives to looking after them.'

4

Dr Pattram's gold bracelets clinked and jangled as she dipped her hand inside the cardboard box on top of her desk. 'These items, Donald, have been removed from your room.'

She held up Don's well-thumbed copy of *Thomas the Tank Engine* with the Fat Controller standing sternly on its cover. She took out his pair of binoculars and train spotter's notebook. She spread out Don's collection of model stations, signals and stretches of railway track. 'It might be a good idea, Donald, for you to try and forget trains for a while.'

Donald ran his toy train determinedly up and down the edge of the doctor's desk as she took out his Thomas the Tank Engine scrapbook and turned over the first page.

'Can you remember this?' Su turned the scrapbook round so Don could read it.

Headless Body Found on Railway Line

A MAN WAS KILLED earlier today after lying on the railway lines in between the carriages of a stationary train. As the train was picking up passengers, the driver failed to spot the fatally-injured man, who has not yet been identified.

The train set off, completely severing the neck of the victim, but the driver, unaware of the incident, continued on his way.

The incident was reported to the police by Donald Valley, a local man who says he witnessed the tragedy when train-spotting in the area.

Says Mr Valley: 'We had to move the body out of the way because the 11.18 InterCity was due at any moment. People ought to be a lot more careful on the railway lines.'

'Can you remember the incident . . . at all?'

As she spoke, Su nudged a large lump of Blu-Tack towards Don in the way that, when she first qualified as a psychiatrist, she might have offered one of her patients a cigarette.

Don picked up the Blu-Tack and began to roll it round his palms.

Su pointed back to the scrapbook. 'There have been other times, haven't there, Don, when you've reported . . . accidents to the police?'

Don tore off wodges of Blu-Tack. His huge thumb pressed heavily, poking and prodding. His fingers squeezed and tore.

'Didn't you report some of these . . .' Su pointed at the scrapbook '. . . other accidents as well?'

Don was making a little blue figure of a man. He held it up and examined it before sitting the man on the edge of Sumitra's desk.

'I wonder if you can remember the first time, the first . . . accident . . .'

Don took another lump of Blu-Tack and made the man a cap, rather like his own train driver's cap.

Su leant forward, lowering her voice. 'I wonder if there might be something . . . something you specially want to tell me, Don. Perhaps about something that happened . . . a long, long time ago . . .'

Gently, almost tenderly, Don picked up the little blue man and laid him along the edge of Sumitra's desk. Then he took the train between his thumb and forefinger, wheeling it along, nearer and nearer. The train paused. Don gritted his teeth.

Su stared. She opened her mouth but said nothing.

Don gripped the plastic train tightly in his fist. His jaw set hard. The veins stood out along his hairy forearms.

He approached the tiny body lying across the track, then swept the train forward with full force. *Crash*. Then back again, bits of Blu-Tack sticking to its wheels. *Crash*. And once again. *Crash*. His huge muscles ironed the body flat, wheeling two deep ridges across its chest. Backwards again, then forwards, a slow rhythm building up.

Su's voice was little more than a whisper as she leant forward as closely as she dared. 'Don,' she asked confidentially. 'Who is it?'

Don's new-found strength was mounting. His eyes flashed wildly at Sumitra. Backwards and forwards, to and fro. The tiny body lay mutilated, no more than a mangled mess.

'Don,' Su asked again, more authoritatively. 'Please try and tell me. It's very important.' She paused. 'Tell me the name of the man.'

The tiny train paused in mid-run as Don cocked his head towards her.

Su fixed her eyes on his with a gaze as cutting as a sharpened axe. 'And,' she ordered, slowly and sternly, 'tell me the name of the driver.'

*

When we've wiped all the breadcrumbs and bits of crisps off our table, we spread out our map of York.

'Well,' Marie slurps through the remnants of her second can of Coke, 'I think we ought to start off with Margaret Clitherow's house because that'll be really boring. Once we've been there, we can just have fun and enjoy ourselves.'

'What about the Bar Convent? That won't be much fun.'

'Oh, I don't know. There's the severed hand.'

I turn the map round. 'Well, we could go on this path

23

by the river.' I trace the footpath with my finger. 'Then across this bridge here . . .'

'And after that, my dear . . .' Marie wags her finger at me '. . . we'll take our first steps down the slippery slope. Lost souls wandering through . . .' she picks up the black glossy brochure and croaks: '"*The North's most infamous horror museum where you can have close encounters of the spine-chilling kind as history is brought frighteningly to life before your very eyes.*"'

I look outside and realize that – as we've been talking – the sky has clouded over. It was bright and sunny when we left. 'You should have brought your big coat,' I tell Marie. 'It might rain when we get there.'

Marie looks down at her thin jacket. She's chosen to wear it because it's brand new, not because it's warm. 'We'll be all right,' she insists. 'The sun'll come out again soon.'

I gaze out at the darkening sky, shadowing the scrapyards, slag heaps and rows of corrugated iron. 'Well, there's no sign of any sun, anywhere.'

But Marie has no interest in the weather. 'I wonder if they'll sell souvenirs.'

'What? At the Dungeon? Like models of people being tortured and everything? Ugh!'

'No, no, I mean, the convent. They might sell replicas of the . . .' she opens her eyes wide with enthusiasm '. . . replicas of the Hand. We could buy loads. We could buy loads and leave them . . .' she squeezes her fists tightly with anticipation, '. . . we could leave one on the counter in the tuck shop.'

I chuckle. 'We could leave them lying about all over school. We could put one in the woodwork room, next to that big saw.'

'We could leave one in the metalwork shop. Or what

about the toilets?' Marie's eyes sparkle with excitement. 'Just imagine a Severed Hand, clawing through the toilet seat!'

'Or it could be reaching out of one of the washbasins.'

'I know.' Marie shifts the map to one side. 'We could make a model of the relic for our project. We could make a sculpture out of papier-mâché.' She exaggerates the artistic sculpting of a severed hand on the table in-between us.

I start to giggle. 'I'll tell you what, we could make it out of sponge cake. We could make it in Cookery and put icing on. We could make pink icing for the fingernails . . .'

'And the blood,' Marie chortles. 'We could have red icing round the bottom for the blood with lengths of red and blue spaghetti sticking out for all the severed veins. Then we could eat it afterwards.'

Both of us mime tucking into a feast of sponge cake, icing, and long lengths of blood-stained spaghetti.

'Can you imagine it standing in the school foyer?'

Our project is supposed to be part of a celebration of all the saints which will culminate in a big exhibition later in the year.

Marie's face lights up as she launches into another of her Sister Frances impersonations. 'And here we have examples of illuminated manuscripts all done by the children with quill pens and calligraphy. We have St Christopher medallions, all hand-forged in Metalwork and what's this . . . ?'

She pretends to pick up the hand and have a nibble. 'Oh yes, very tasty. A nice, light, spongy mixure, well-risen, with a smooth almond paste spread with royal icing . . .'

'Can I see your tickets, please?'

Both Marie and I are collapsing into fits of giggles as a very large ticket inspector with a broad Yorkshire accent looms towards our table.

Marie unfastens her rucksack once again and, as I glance up, I notice for the first time that large white snowflakes are falling past the window.

5

'It's never startin' to snow.'

'What do you reckon it is, then? An extra-large angel with a very bad case of dandruff?'

The first white flakes flurried past the cab in which Les Carr was, as usual, driving the 9.23 Wednesday morning train from Sheffield to York which stopped at most of the stations along the way.

Les had left the green dome of Meadowhall behind. He'd passed underneath the Tinsley viaduct with its giant, concrete, twin gas holders. He'd sped beyond to the Blackburn Meadows sewage works. He'd stopped at Rotherham Central and Swinton. And now, with a flutter of excitement, he was easing along the stretch towards the Railway Tavern at Moorthorpe station.

'Well, this is where we'll be tonight.' Ken, his senior conductor, inclined his head towards the pub.

Les nodded confidently. Within the last few days he'd acquired the determined look of a relegation-zone team-manager just before the last match of the season.

'P'r'aps they'll be put off by t'bad weather,' Ken suggested hopefully. 'We might win by default, eh?'

Les bit his bottom lip. He actually realized it would take a lot more than a flurry of snow to keep the Jolly Rogers – three times prizewinners of the John Sanella quiz league – at home on the night of the final.

'Here we are.'

Les took a childish delight in pulling out the throttle and giving an extra loud whistle as the Sprinter rattled through the station. The Railway Tavern was actually the old railway station waiting room transformed into a pub. This was where, that very evening, the finals of the John Sanella Quiz League were due to be taking place.

'There's not much chance o' that lot not turnin' up,' Les remarked. 'They've all got loads o' money. They'll all have Range Rovers – four-wheel drives an' that.'

'Or they'll send for a taxi.'

'They'll be used to snow as well. They probably go skiin' for their 'olidays.'

'Probably all got a spare set o' skis in their garages.'

'Conservatories,' Les corrected.

They both laughed.

Les and Ken's rivals in the John Sanella final were three well-known boffins – a senior librarian, an engineering consultant and an assistant professor – named the Jolly Rogers after a very famous flag.

And pitted against them were the rank outsiders – a senior conductor, an engine driver and an assistant nurse – named the Flying Scotsmen after a very famous locomotive.

'Do you think we're in with a chance, then?' Ken asked, leaning slightly as Les took the curve.

'Don't see why not. We've done all right so far.'

Of course the Flying Scotsmen, who weren't particularly brainy, had never intended to go in for the quiz. It had all started when Ken's brother and his wife were staying in Wath over Christmas and they'd all gone down to The Grapes for a celebration drink. They'd been sitting with Carter, a young lad who was a nurse in a mental hospital. It was Whitely, Ken Wood's sister-in-law who suggested joining in the pub's special Christmas quiz. As the couple had just flown down from Scotland, they decided to call their team the Flying Scotsmen.

The Sprinter headed north towards the Ferrybridge

power station, belching steam across the river. 'Can you see that chimney,' Les pointed out to Ken, 'over between that clump o' trees?'

'Where?'

'Looks a bit like an old castle.'

'Oh yeah.'

'That's where Carter Knowle works. He was tellin' me about it last week. St Aiden's, they call it. Some right characters apparently.

'Oh aye.'

'Apparently there's one poor bloke in there spends all day long pretendin' he's a train.'

*

The runaway train came down the track and she blew, whooo . . .

Don's Blu-Tack man was now a mangled mess, a blue splodge flattened against the edge of Dr Pattram's desk.

'You see, my theory is, Donald, that it's not just trains that fascinate you, but train crashes.'

The runaway train came down the track and she blew, whooo . . .

Don sang quietly to himself as he picked at the shreds of Blu-Tack clinging to the underside of his model engine.

'I'm beginning to wonder if what you're trying to do is re-enact train crashes everywhere you go. With the wheelie bin, with the lawn mower, with the tea trolley . . .'

Don said nothing.

Su leant forward confidentially. 'Do you know who I am, Donald?'

Don picked at the Blu-Tack, wiping the wheels clean with his chubby fingers.

29

Su took a deep breath as the silence strained between them like a long, long string of overstretched Blu-Tack. 'I'm a doctor.'

Don was unimpressed.

'Can you remember what I explained to you – about doctors?'

Silence.

'Doctors are here to help make people better.'

Don scratched the last of the Blu-Tack from his wheels.

'You see, Don, each one of us has a myriad world of different characters hidden deep inside us. We can only really express our characters one at a time. So one of the characters you express is that of the train driver. And the train – that's a character – a kind of role you play – as well. But you have other unexplored characters. Each of us, for instance, has a doctor hidden deep inside us – we all have the ability to make ourselves well. We can use that doctor to heal ourselves.'

Don grinned.

'So,' Sumitra closed the scrapbook and slapped it down on the desk. 'We're going to try a little experiment, Donald. We're going to try and live without our trains and see how we get on.' She returned the book to its cardboard box. 'No more train spotting.' She plonked the binoculars down on top.

Carter, still waiting over by the door, stared at her open-mouthed.

'No more model railways.' Su threw in the model stations and lengths of railway track.

'But . . .'

Sumitra glowered at Carter.

He took a deep breath and said nothing.

'You see, if you forget about all your trains for a while,

30

Donald,' Sumitra continued, 'it will give you a chance to come to terms with reality.'

Don fingered one of the buttons on his old-fashioned train driver's uniform.

'You can stop pretending that you're a train and start to remember who you really are.' She placed the lid on top of the cardboard box and pressed it firmly down. 'For the time being,' she explained to Carter, 'we need to keep Don in a private ward away from other patients.' She offered him the box. 'You can lock that up somewhere safe.'

There was a pause. 'I'm sorry, Dr Pattram . . .' Carter shook his head '. . . but these are Don's possessions. I mean, well, he treasures them. I don't really think we've got any right to . . .'

'Nurse Knowle, this is no time for sentimentality.' Su shoved the box firmly towards him. 'Take these away and lock them somewhere safe.'

Carter reluctantly walked over to the desk and picked up the cardboard carton.

Sumitra nodded towards the door. 'I'll give you a call in half an hour when it's time to take Donald back.'

6

Sumitra straightened her sari across her shoulder and folded her manicured fingers upon her lap. 'We were talking about the train driver . . .'

Don stared at the floor.

'I know the memories might be painful, Donald, but, if we talk about things, it often helps to . . .'

Don turned and looked up. He had the exhausted expression of a man who had just completed a very long journey. He opened his mouth and spoke slowly. 'This train,' he announced sadly, 'is an InterCity 125.'

Su stroked the heavy rings encircling her long, smooth fingers. 'I wondered if there might have been an accident involving . . . someone that you knew . . .'

'This train . . .' Don's voice became more strong and certain '. . . is mechanically sound.' Suddenly he leant forward and thumped his clenched fist down on the doctor's desk. 'It is unnecessary for this train to be taken in for locomotive repairs.'

Su said nothing.

Don stood up to face her. His jaw set hard and the line of tattoos round his neck pulsed and quivered. 'This train . . .' Don spoke slowly and authoritatively '. . . is not a slow goods train. This is an InterCity 125.'

Su motioned towards the chair. 'Sit down, Donald.'

Reluctantly, Don collapsed back upon his chair. The air was taut with silence.

Su waited. Don appeared to be slumping into lethargy. The tension eased.

'I think you've been trying to tell me something quite important, Donald, haven't you?'

Her patient stared at the floor.

'This little man with the train driver's cap . . . ?'

Don still did not look up.

'*Was* it a train driver's cap?'

Don began to rock very, very slowly, backwards and fowards on his seat.

'You made a little man with Blu-Tack and then you sat him by the railway line, didn't you?'

Don began to breathe heavily. He rocked harder, backwards and forwards . . . backwards and forwards.

'The man was lying on the railway line when the train came along . . .'

Pause.

'. . . wasn't he?'

The rocking increased. The legs of the chair rose and clattered, backwards and forwards. Backwards and forwards. Don breathed heavily, his cheeks flushed red.

'You were going to tell me the name of the man, Donald . . . weren't you . . . ?'

Don's eyes opened wide. He clenched his hairy fists, his knuckles protruding, white and hard. Suddenly, he leapt to his feet, towering over Sumitra.

Su glanced towards the phone, just beyond her reach on the far side of her desk.

Don opened his mouth wide as if he were going to scream but the sound Su heard was a low, deep gurgling. The sound of a man who was drowning. He held tightly to the back of his chair, his knuckles pale and taut. There was a moment's pause before Don picked up the plastic chair, held it poised above his head, then *crash!* He flung it across the room.

Su reached for the phone.

Don raised his huge arm and swiped it across the desk, scattering boxes of paperclips and Blu-Tack, pencils and drawing pins. Just as Su was reaching out for the telephone, Don grabbed it from her, raised it in the air then smashed it against the wall.

'What . . .' Su sprang out of her seat and leapt towards the door.

Don's eyes were blazing. Beads of sweat glistened on his forehead. He blocked Sumitra's route to the door as he pounded his huge fists on the edge of her desk. 'Loxley Valley,' he shouted angrily, 'was the driver of an InterCity 125.'

Sumitra shrank back against the wall.

Don towered to his full height, jabbing his forefinger towards his chest. 'This train . . .' he spoke in slow, considered tones, 'is an InterCity 125.' He narrowed his eyes with fury. 'This train is not in need of routine maintenance.'

Su sidled back behind her desk.

Don spoke again more loudly and slowly. 'This train is *not* in need of repair.'

Sumitra nodded politely. She glanced towards the door. She'd just decided to make a run for it when, to her horror, Don began to clamber on top of her desk. Suddenly he lunged towards her, grabbing the edge of her sari.

'Aaagh!' Su let out a scream. She was extremely thankful that the weather had been so cold, as it meant that she was fully clothed underneath her sari. She backed away as Don grabbed the red silk, tearing it from its clasp.

Su screamed again as her sari fell to the floor. The last thing she remembered was the sight of Don with his massive, bear-like hands, lunging towards her from the top of her desk.

34

'They keep 'em on tranquillisers nowadays so they're easy to look after. They don't cause any trouble, then.'

Les drove past a level crossing, through grassy fields, closer towards the copse of trees and the castellated tower.

'Well, I wouldn't care for Carter's job,' Ken observed. 'I 'ave enough on lookin' after passengers. They're enough to drive anybody round the bend.'

Les began to apply the brakes as he saw a red light glowing in the distance. 'What I'm sayin' is that they're all on drugs nowadays.'

'What? Passengers?'

'No, no. Folks in mental 'ospitals.'

Ken nodded, gazing out at the passing flakes of snow as the train slowed down. 'I've been thinkin' about our Whitely.'

'Why? Is she on drugs?'

'No, no. I mean for the quiz.'

'Oh, I see.'

At the Christmas Quiz in The Grapes of Wath, Whitely had answered questions on Geography, History and Music while Ken and Les had got the beer in. Then Whitely answered all the questions on Ornithology, Botany and Computers while Carter and Les got more beer in. When Ken and Carter went to queue up for last orders, Whitely answered questions on Films, General Knowledge and Geology.

'We could have done with her comin' down again tonight.'

Afterwards, the Flying Scotsmen discovered that not only had they won two gallons of free beer but, having the highest score of the season, they were through to the next round of the quiz.

'Now then, lads,' Granville, the quizmaster, had asked

them in the next round, 'can anyone tell me the name of a road that cuts between two mountains?'

But once Whitely was back in Inverness, the Flying Scotsmen were flummoxed. Les was quite well up on Geography – provided it was places on a train route and within a fifty-mile radius of Sheffield, but he wasn't too familiar with mountains. He shook his head. 'How about you, Carter?'

With all the eyes of The Grapes upon him, Carter Knowle had tried to look intelligent. He'd rested his head on his chin, stroking an imaginary beard. 'I'll have to give it some thought.'

'How about you, Ken?'

Ken searched his brain. He took a long swig of beer to try and give him further inspiration. In the end, he just shook his head. 'Pass.'

'Correct. A road that goes between two mountains is called a pass. And that gives the first point to the Flying Scotsmen.'

'Well done, lads.'

7

We arrive in York to find no sign of snow. Although there's a biting wind that sends a shiver through our bones, the sky is clear and the pavements are dry. 'There you are, you see,' says Marie, huddled inside her thin jacket. 'What did I tell you?

I don't say anything. We stand outside the railway station, searching for the right way into town.

'When we got off the train, I thought we'd be *here*,' Marie complains.

'We are here.'

'No. No, we're not. We're miles away. We can't even see York Minster let alone the Dungeon and the shops and everything.'

Just next to the station is a low building:

York's Biggest Smallest Attraction.

'What's that?'

'I don't know. Some kind of model railway. We don't want to go in there,' Marie says scathingly.

I actually like model railways. I have two younger brothers and a little sister and all of them are really keen on model trains. 'Well, we could just go in and have a warm while we look at the map again.'

Marie takes a long, deep breath and sighs.

The Biggest Smallest Attraction turns out to be a lot more than a model railway. As we walk through into the darkness, our eyes begin to focus on an entire, miniature world.

'Oh, look at that. Isn't it good?' As well as the trains and stations, there are houses, a church and a farm . . . all in perfect proportion.

'There's a farmyard. Look, can you see the sheep? And the pigs. Can you see the tiny piglets?' I marvel at the teeny-weeny piglets and at the minute figures clinging hold of their microscopic parcels as they stand on the platforms and wait for their miniature trains.

'Mmm.' Marie doesn't sound enthusiastic.

'Oh, it's brilliant.'

'Actually, Teresa, we've come to York to see the Dungeon. That's my idea of something brilliant.'

Of course, Marie is unimpressed with the miniature people because none of them are sliced in half or roasted alive. All of them, in fact, are completely intact with no sign of dripping blood or severed limbs. A teeny man raises a flag the size of a ladybird's handkerchief up on its flagpole; he isn't hung or garrotted or left dangling inside a gibbet.

'There's a Punch and Judy, look. And a tiny, weeny, miniature train.'

Marie sighs. 'Mm. Exciting isn't it?'

No one gets hurt. Everything moves like clockwork. Nothing happens unexpectedly. The trains purr past at their appointed times; none of them crash or go flying off the rails. A helicopter winches a tiny swimmer out of the water. He hovers for a few seconds then is gently lowered back. 'The twins would love this.'

'Yes, Teresa; that's because they're only seven years old.'

I gaze in fascination at the microscopic train running inside the miniature railway. I watch the windmill's sails rotate and peer at the children whirling round and round on carousels and Ferris wheels. And then I'm aware of a very large person looming close behind me.

'Look, there's Thomas the Tank Engine.' I point out the old-fashioned blue train with its round, bright eyes

38

and familiar smiling face. 'The twins have one just like that.'

Marie gives an exaggerated yawn.

'And that's the Fat Controller.' I show her the tubby figure with his smart black jacket and yellow waistcoat.

A large figure lopes towards the rail, edging me out of the way.

I glance up. There's a very large woman wearing a red and black sari. As she takes up a space that would normally be occupied by two, she isn't all that easy to miss.

Suddenly the room darkens. The display lights dim. The whole of the landscape changes. As the main lights are extinguished, tiny little specks – as frail as fireflies – light up the houses, the trains and the streetlamps. 'Look. They're making it night-time now.'

Standing close beside me, the Asian woman leans over the display, blocking my view.

While I'm waiting for her to move, I point out the different trains to Marie. 'I think that green train there's called Percy,' I explain. 'There's this story where he's left out all night by himself.'

Marie nods without a great deal of enthusiasm. She leans her bag beside the rail and fishes inside it for the map.

The woman beside me is still leaning over the Thomas the Tank Engine display. She raises her hand for a moment as though she's about to reach inside the rail.

'Oh,' Marie complains, 'I wish they'd put the lights back on. I can't see the map.'

The woman's face isn't easy to distinguish because it's hidden inside her sari. I assume, of course, that she's Asian, but what surprises me as she reaches forward are her shoes – or, well, her boots.

Marie is concentrating on her map. 'There. I've got it now.' She presses her finger on the map as the lights begin to brighten. 'Look, we need to go on this road here beside the river.'

The tiny house and streetlights dim to nothing as daylight slowly returns. I glance back at the woman's feet. She's wearing a pair of heavy black boots. Like Doc Martens. I shake my head. All the Asian ladies I know normally wear sandals. They sometimes have nice embroidery on, but I've never seen an Asian lady wearing boots before – not with a sari anyway.

The woman seems aware of the fact that I'm staring rather rudely at her and draws back.

Marie's already heading towards the exit. 'Well, that was boring,' she announces as I follow her into the souvenir shop.

'I thought it was good.'

'Well, you've got no taste, have you?'

'Just because there was nothing gory. It was just nice, that's all. It was really well-made. If the twins were here, they'd have enjoyed it.'

Marie raises her eyebrows as she examines the souvenirs. 'Well, here's your favourite friend again, Teresa,' she scoffs. She points to a Thomas the Tank Engine display. 'Look, you can buy all your special activity books here. And your key-rings, drinking glasses, mugs and all your colouring books.'

I do actually think Thomas the Tank Engine activity books would make very good presents for the twins and they don't cost too much money. 'Anyway,' I lower my voice, 'did you see that woman in the sari?'

Marie nods.

I bring my voice down to a whisper. 'Did you see her boots?'

'No. Why?'

I glance over my shoulder but the shop assistant is hovering just behind us. 'I'll tell you later.'

I pick up a couple of Thomas the Tank Engine story books and take them to the counter together with the two activity books.

Just then, a man puts his head round the door that leads to the railway. 'I'll have to leave you on your own for a few minutes,' he explains to the shop girl.

'Is anything wrong?' She beds down my books in their carrier.

'I don't know.' The man frowns. 'I just can't understand it. It's never happened before – three of the trains have just crashed.'

8

'Well, so long as we're all right for gettin' to the pub,' remarked Ken, sitting with Les in the station canteen. 'I'm a bit bothered about this snow.'

'Oh, we've got plenty of time,' answered Les, dusting the white flakes off his sleeve. 'We're due back in Sheffield at 18.16. Half an hour to get washed an' changed an' have something to eat, then an hour's plenty for gettin' to the pub.'

'If you're pushed for time, you can always get something to eat up there. They've got a good chip shop just down the road.'

'Well, we should be all right. So long as we don't run into heavy snowdrifts . . .' Les grinned.

'Or frozen points,' added Ken.

'Or thick fog.'

'Or last year's leaves blowin' on the line.'

'Best hear the weather forecast, anyhow.' Ken glanced at his watch. He turned towards the canteen assistant, draining chips in a wire basket. 'Would you mind turnin' the wireless up? We want to 'ear the weather forecast.'

The radio crackled above the sizzling of the chips and the belching tea urn.

And here is a snow warning. Snow is forecast for many parts of the area later on today. This could be heavy at times with a chance of drifting on high ground. Temperatures are expected to fall below freezing. Motorists are advised to take extreme care as road conditions could be treacherous . . .

'How about rail conditions, then?' asked Ken. 'Are they gonna be treacherous or what?'

. . . And now over to the local news desk. Police are searching for a psychiatric patient who escaped earlier today from St Aiden's hospital near York.

It is believed that the mental patient, Donald Valley, aged twenty-eight, tied up and gagged a hospital psychiatrist before escaping with the keys to one of the cars in the staff car park. The car was later found abandoned near York station.

The missing man is white, heavily-built, about six foot three inches tall with a skinhead haircut and a row of tattoos round his neck. He was last seen wearing a train driver's uniform. A spokesman from the hospital says that the patient is dangerous and should on no account be approached by members of the public.

Anyone who thinks they might have seen this man should get in touch with local police immediately.

*

We open the exit doors of the model railway, then stand and stare in amazement. We must have been inside the exhibition for less than half an hour but that's all it's taken for the landscape to be totally transformed. Pavements, roofs, cars, bus stops, railings – everything is covered in a soft and frosty film of snow.

'Oh, that's pretty.'

But Marie has already set off skating down the pavement. Arms stretched wide, she slides and slithers.

Oh, I've got my skates on with Jesus . . .
she carols.

I skid forward and grab hold of her hand. I reach out

my other arm to steady myself, waving my carrier in the
air as we slide along together:

I'm going skating with the Lord . . .

We raise our arms to form a bridge as we slither past a
group of children queuing for the model railway. They
giggle and duck their heads as we slide past.

With Jesus on the ice,
We'll soon be in Paradise . . .

we chorus:

Oh-h-h, yes, we're going skating with the Lo-o-ord.

When we eventually find the centre of York, the streets
are narrow and twisty and cobbled and they don't seem
to bear much relation to the clearly-marked streets on
our map. There are lots of signposts pointing to the main
attractions, but by now most of the writing is hidden by
snow. And, of course, it's much too cold to keep standing still and checking the route. We just slither along in
what we think is the right direction.

We find the path by the side of the river but there's a
huge gale blowing so we have to huddle close to the tall
buildings to try and keep dry. It takes us about fifteen
minutes to find the place where Margaret Clitherow used
to live, The Shambles.

'Oh, look at that.'

'Isn't it pretty?'

'Just like a Christmas card.'

The old-fashioned buildings, sparkling with snow,
remind me of the pictures in a story book I used to have.
'It's like *A Christmas Carol*,' I tell Marie.

'Which one?'

'You know, *A Christmas Carol*.'

'Si-i-lent night,' warbles Marie, sliding along the pavement, 'ho-o-ly night . . .'

It's a shame the weather's turned so cold because what I'd really like to do is explore The Shambles properly – to investigate all the higgledy-piggledy souvenir shops and cafés and the market stalls round the back.

'All is calm, all is bright . . .'

My first impression is that we've gone back in time – everything is so old-fashioned. The street is very narrow but it gets even narrower with the houses really close together at the top. If you lived in one of the attics, I'm sure you could actually reach out and pass something to the person who lived across the street. You could even shake hands with them.

'It'd be good to live up there.'

'I could live on one side,' says Marie, 'and you could live on the other and then, when you were making a mug of coffee, you could pass one across to me.'

'And you could pass me your homework so we could both check all our answers.'

'And you could give me a shout in the morning so I wouldn't be late for school.'

Most of the buildings have black, exposed, wooden beams and many of the shop windows are made from tiny, old-fashioned, square panes of glass.

'There's Margaret Clitherow's.'

We leave the street just as we're starting to get really soaked by the snow.

'Well,' says Marie as we push open the heavy wooden door. 'Let's just hope that, before she set off to be squashed to death by the rocks, our friend Maggie forgot to turn the central heating off.'

9

'DOWN, DOWN TO YOUR DOOM . . .' an echoing voice shrieks out in warning, as we shiver past a black-hooded skull pinioned to the wall.

'It's more like a ghost train than a museum.' I cling tightly to Marie's snow-soaked sleeve as we stumble down the staircase.

ENTER AT YOUR PERIL

are the words scrawled upon blackened stone.

'It's a bit dark.'

'I know.'

The walls of the Dungeon are cold and bare with slabs of stone on the floor. At the foot of the gloomy staircase, accompanied by deep, booming rolls of thunder, we await our turn to pay.

'Just one?'

I gaze up at the huge, manacled skeleton lounging on top of the nearby toilet block and realize that I'm shivering – partly with cold and partly with excitement as Marie and I cling to each other's snowy sleeves.

We're waiting for the woman in front but she just stares at the skeleton as if he's a long-lost friend. She seems very similar to the Asian lady we saw in the miniature railway.

DOWN TO YOUR DOOM! DOWN TO YOUR DOOM!

I give Marie a little nudge.

'Is there just one of you?' asks the cashier.

Although it's too dark to see her properly, the Asian

woman is so large that you'd be unlikely to mistake her. I'm amazed as well that she doesn't have a coat. Her sari must be soaked.

When there's no reply, the cashier asks again, 'Just one?'

Marie and I both stand back to make it clear that we're not with the strange lady when suddenly she starts to speak. She has an unusual high-pitched voice. 'We all have a myriad world of different characters hidden deep inside us . . .' she explains to the cashier.

Marie and I exchange glances.

'. . . we can only really express them one at a time.'

The woman at the cash desk looks a bit confused. 'One adult,' she says uncertainly and slides a ticket forward.

She's shaking her head in confusion as Marie and I press forward with our money.

DOWN TO YOUR DOOM! DOWN TO YOUR DOOM!

I glance ahead towards the dim passageway where the Asian woman is striding along in her Doc Martens and I think about turning back. I wasn't expecting the Dungeon to be pleasant but I wasn't expecting it to be quite as sinister as this.

'Come on, Teresa, pull out your ticket. Pull yourself together.'

Of course, I know how much Marie has been looking forward to the Dungeon. I can't leave her in here on her own.

'Come on, then. *Down . . . down to our Dooom!*' Marie grabs hold of my arm and drags me forward into the darkness.

It takes a long time for our eyes to adjust as we stumble along the narrow passage. The only lights are flickering through the eyes of skeletons and skulls.

'Good isn't it?'

I say nothing.

The dank air resounds with the harmonies of a choir of chanting monks.

'Well,' says Marie brightly, 'We should have invited Sister Frances; she'd have enjoyed this holy music.' But of course, as we step into the grim interior, there are no chanting monks, just disembodied, echoing voices and the deep, rhythmical tolling of a funeral bell.

The first exhibit is disgusting. It makes me want to vomit. It's called Daneskin. The notice explains how the early Christians used to skin their Viking enemies alive and nail their skins to church doors. 'How could anybody do anything so horrible?' I ask in disbelief, staring at the dried and stretched patch of human skin.

But Marie just looks highly impressed. 'It says they did it as a warning not to stray from Christianity.'

'But that means they did it in the name of religion.'

Marie just smiles and nods. 'I know.'

We creep along the dismal corridor, still clinging tightly to each other's arms. 'Oh, look! The Gibbet,' Marie announces. 'That's good, isn't it?'

We stand and gaze at a decomposed body, in tattered rags, dangling in its cage. '"*Following trial and hanging*,"' I read, '"*the criminal's body was placed in a man-sized metal cage and hung from the gibbet as a grisly deterrent to others . . .*"'

I swallow hard. 'Just imagine walking past one of those on your way to school.'

Marie carries on: '"Samuel Pepys wrote of passing a body in a gibbet cage which had been hanging in the same spot for over a year."'

'Well, it's as well we didn't invite Sister Frances,' I grin. 'It'd have given her some suggestions for what to do with people who stuck chewing gum underneath the tables in the dining room.'

'She'd have one hanging in every classroom,' Marie chuckles, wagging her finger. 'Now there's a lesson to you all, everyone. Never stick chewing gum underneath the tables or under your chair seats.'

We steal round the corner to the sound of stretching and groaning and encounter a hapless victim being torn apart on The Rack. The automatous torturers pull on their poles as we approach, cranking the machine.

'I wonder if they come out a lot taller and thinner than when they went it?' Marie muses as we listen to the anguished groans and creaks. 'Just think, if Bernadette Dronfield heard about it, she'd ask if she could have a go.'

'She'd emerge twice as tall with a body like a beanpole.'

After The Guillotine and The Stocks, there's Beheading. The display shows a hooded executioner fiendishly wiping his axe blade beside the blood-soaked stump of a neck. In its nest of straw before us, the decapitated head twitches intermittently.

Suddenly, the large woman in the sari appears in front of us. She steps towards the head twitching in its basket and, to our amazement, speaks to it. Her voice is the same high-pitched squeak that we heard before. 'Each one of us has a doctor hidden deep inside us,' she warbles to the severed head.

I walk closer to Marie and hold tightly to her arm.

'We can use that doctor to heal ourselves.'

Marie loosens her arm from mine and discreetly wiggles her finger against the side of her head.

'Doctors are here to help make people better.'

I nod and say nothing.

We both try politely to ignore the strange woman and walk across to read the notice. 'The Earl of Northumberland. Wasn't he supposed to have inspired Margaret Clitherow?'

'Was he?' I can't honestly imagine anybody being much inspired by the sight of the horrible spurts of crimson blood, the severed larynx and rolling eye-balls.

'I think so. Sister told us how Margaret Clitherow saw his head spiked on top of a gate at the end of her street and decided that she wanted to be a martyr.'

'What did she do that for?'

'I don't know.'

We both read: '"*For the 'crime' of attempting to place Mary Queen of Scots on the English throne, the Earl of Northumberland was convicted of treason and beheaded in York city centre in 1572. He was seen as a martyr and onlookers soaked their handkerchiefs in his blood*".'

I gaze down at the blood-matted, severed head. 'That's what she asked us, isn't it?'

'What?'

'Who was responsible for Margaret's death?'

The head twitches uncomfortably. 'Well, you can't blame him, poor chap,' Marie insists. 'He was only an ornament on the gatepost.'

As we move on, our eyes become more accustomed to the dark. There aren't many other people looking round; a girl and her boyfriend arm-in-arm, a couple of Japanese tourists, and the large Asian woman whose face we still can't see.

'Well, here's our friend Maggie.'

The portrayal of Margaret Clitherow makes her look quite glamorous. She has a slender, shapely body, a pale complexion and long hair spread out like a mermaid's across the stone slabs.

'She looks quite nice.'

Unfortunately, Margaret's martyrdom is accompanied by the sound of her awful groans together with the splintering of bones bursting from her skin as the rocks are piled above her.

'Bursting with health, my dear,' Marie chuckles. 'Bursting with enthusiasm.'

'Bursting with kindness.'

Marie reads the notice out loud. '"It took her a quarter of an hour to die."'

'Ugh.'

'"*Margaret Clitherow's crime was harbouring Catholic priests during the Reformation in the sixteenth century.*"' Marie points to the leering rogue piling on the rocks. 'Anyway, I think he's the one responsible for Margaret's death. If he hadn't insisted on building his rockery just in the spot where she was having a lie-down . . .'

We both chuckle.

Of course, the large woman in the sari has to say her bit to Margaret Clitherow as well. We step swiftly out of the way as she elbows forward. She pauses, her face still hidden from view, and gazes down at Margaret's broken, gasping form. 'You know how sometimes people break into pieces . . . ?' she asks the blood-streaked, groaning body. 'Everything . . . well . . . we all break down sometimes . . .'

10

'Did you report some of these . . . accidents?'

Marie and I exchange glances but say nothing as the large Asian lady pushes me out of the way. I'm quite taken aback to find how strong she is. In fact she almost knocks me flying into a large, obnoxious, blood-stained pool. I'm just reading the neatly-typed notice about Death by Drowning. It explains how victims were chained to the riverbank to await the next tide when they'd be eaten alive by the starving, needle-toothed rats we can see lurking in the shadows. Below me floats a poor chap with his arms in chains and all of a sudden, with a nudge in the back from our Asian friend, I almost topple down to join him. I regain my balance just as the disgusting blood-bath suddenly spouts up, gurgling and swishing round.

'I'm sorry, Teresa. This is no time to jump in the Jacuzzi.' Marie drags me back by the arm. 'And anyway, there's a young man in there already.'

The Indian lady approaches the poor chap who's quickly being submerged as the water rises menacingly. 'I wonder if there might have been an accident . . . involving someone that you knew . . .'

Marie and I step swiftly out of the way.

'I know the memories might be painful but, if you can talk about them . . .'

All around us, the air resounds with wailing and groaning, sawing and cleaving. There's the rhythmical clank of the gears which turn The Wheel on which a sorrowful victim spins out the last few minutes of his life.

There's the weary sawing of two chainmail-clad jailers slicing their way through the partly-cleaved body of St George.

'I wonder what's in there.'

The Indian lady has disappeared inside a wooden door, closing it shut behind her. Marie and I walk across.

THE GUNPOWDER PLOT

'Well, this looks very educational.' Marie places her hand on the door handle.

'Hang on a minute.'

From inside, there's the muffled sound of a tape-recorded commentary. I read the notice on the door. 'We've got to wait until it stops,' I explain.

'What do you mean?'

'It says here. Look. "Please wait until the programme has finished before you enter. Then press the green button to start the presentation."'

'Well, that woman didn't wait, did she?'

That's true. 'Perhaps she didn't see the notice.'

'We'll wait for her to come out, then.'

While we're waiting, we watch a glamorous creature being roasted in a cauldron hung above a fire of glowing coals. 'If Sister Frances were here, she'd be giving us a talk on the persistent portrayal of women as victims in society,' Marie observes as the cauldron bubbles beside her.

'If Sister Frances were here, she'd have complained to the authorities straight away and had the whole place closed down by now.'

Marie bends down to listen at the door of the Guy

Fawkes exhibition. 'Oh, come on,' she complains impatiently. 'Hurry up.'

I lean with my ear next to the door.

Silence.

'Do you think it's finished?'

We both bend down and listen.

More silence.

'Well, if it's over, why hasn't that woman come out?'

I gaze at the black-cloaked Reaper, stalking across the ceiling with his bony jaw and long-handled scythe. 'Perhaps she wants to hear it all again. Perhaps she missed the first bit.'

Marie nods. 'Come on, then we'd better go in.'

I glance up at the Reaper's blood-shot eyes, glowing like red sparks from underneath his hooded cloak. I take a deep breath as we open the door and walk inside.

*

FAX FROM:

Notre Dame Catholic School
Malin Bridge
Sheffield

Headteacher: Sister Frances

To:
St Aiden's Hospital, near York.

Please will you inform Agnes Ranmoor
that Sister Frances will be able to visit
her after all at her usual time this afternoon.

    Interviews at the school have finished
early so Sister will be on her way shortly.
If Dr Pattram would like to discuss
Sister's proposals for leading the patients
in selected groups for silent meditation
and psalm recital, Sister will be happy to
stay on and make arrangements with her.

With love and very best wishes,

Crystal Peaks

School Secretary

The wooden door closes behind us. The room is pitch black. Marie and I cling tightly to each other.

We seem to be standing in a large, empty space. I peer around but all I can see is darkness. I screw the sleeve of Marie's jacket tightly in my fist. I open my mouth to speak but then close it again. We edge back slowly towards the safety of the door.

I reach out and grope for the door handle, then notice a green button on the wall. 'It says "press the button".'

'What button?'

'Here. Look.'

I reach behind Marie and press the illuminated green spot on the wall. We stand, staring, watching, until the darkness lifts. A loudspeaker crackles in a far corner of the room. The Gunpowder Plot splutters into life.

A chorus of children's voices starts to chant:

Remember, remember, the fifth of November . . .

At the far end of the room, a small bonfire stacked with wood, begins to blaze:

gunpowder, treason and plot . . .

The glow of the fire enables us to see more clearly.

I see no reason why gunpowder treason
should ever be forgot.

The room isn't as big as I thought. There's a square in the middle for the audience – empty except for Marie and myself – then, round the edges, are the tableaux, enclosed behind a kind of thin net screen.

The light brightens on the tableau to our left. A group of men are standing round a table, scrutinising plans on a large sheet of paper.

'James I was making life in England impossible for Catholics,' the commentator tells us. He goes on to explain about the various conspirators who wanted to kill the king so they could put Elizabeth's daughter, Mary, on the throne.

The conspirators are wearing old-fashioned clothes with big, wide-brimmed hats, white ruff collars, doublets and leggings.

'Guy Fawkes was not the leader of the plot,' the commentator explains, 'but was chosen to help the conspirators because of his knowledge of gunpowder.'

What's puzzling me, of course, is nothing to do with the conspirators and why they wanted to blow up Parliament. What's puzzling me is what on earth has happened to the Asian woman in the sari.

The first tableau begins to fade and, on the other side of the room, another scene lights up, showing the cellars and the stash of gunpowder. We see the figure of Guy Fawkes as he's discovered beneath the Houses of Parliament.

I give Marie a bit of a nudge, but she's just staring at the barrels of gunpowder as Guy Fawkes prepares to turn Parliament into the biggest firework display of all time.

Could she have sneaked out, perhaps, while we were watching the woman roasting in the cauldron? It doesn't seem very likely. We never moved more than a few metres from the door.

'That woman.' I nudge Marie again. 'Where's she gone?'

Marie purses her lips and glances round. 'She must have gone out.' She nods towards the back of the room. 'Perhaps there's another door.'

I look all round but I can't see another door. There isn't anything else in the room apart from the Guy Fawkes tableaux and us.

We hear about the interrogation of Guy Fawkes and

his refusal to name the others involved in the conspiracy. Needless to say, the poor man has to endure several days of torment as the authorities try to extract the names of the other conspirators from him. The scene with the gunpowder fades and another tableau lights up. A small door opens to show the torture chamber with Guy Fawkes tied down on a slab.

We can see the torturer and Guy Fawkes. I don't really want to watch all the details; I feel as though I've seen enough scenes of cruelty and horror to last me the rest of my life. I'm just about to close my eyes, when I find myself blinking instead. 'Who's that?' I whisper.

Standing at the rear of the torture chamber is another man. He isn't dressed like all the others; he's wearing a dark-coloured uniform and his hair is very short. He doesn't seem to fit in with the scene at all.

I rub my eyes. 'Who's that supposed to be? I whisper again.

Marie shakes her head. 'I don't know.'

To everyone's relief, Guy Fawkes finally gives way to torture and names the other conspirators. Marie and I stand, still clinging to each other's arms, as the judge describes a list of punishments so disgusting they bring the taste of this morning's breakfast back into my throat. He obviously intends to discourage anyone else from trying to blow up Parliament for the next few thousand years. But I still can't take my eyes off the large man standing at the back. He has huge shoulders and a skin-head haircut and . . . just then, he moves. Not a lot, just a fraction. His eyes blink and his head twitches.

'He's just moved,' I whisper.

'What?'

'That man.' I nudge Marie again. 'He's just moved.'

Marie looks across but the man is standing perfectly

still. I stare at him hard. He's very large and fat with black marks in a row round his neck. The light begins to fade. I crane my neck forward and, just in the tiny split second before the lights go out, he does it again. He blinks.

I swallow hard and edge back towards the door. I tug Marie by the sleeve. I whisper very quietly. 'He's moved again.'

'You what?' Marie bends her ear down close to my lips.

'His eyes just flickered.'

'Are you sure?'

I just can't understand it. Why would a real person pretend to be someone in a torture chamber? Why would they be standing here in the darkness with all the models and . . .

Remember, remember the fifth of November . . . chant the children's voices once again as I turn and grope for the door handle. I actually find my hands slipping off it because my palms are so damp with sweat.

I open the door at last and both of us breathe out a sigh of relief. There's something almost reassuring about the horrors of the Dungeon and the crowd of eager faces all waiting their turn to experience The Gunpowder Plot for themselves.

★

ST AIDEN'S HOSPITAL
NEAR YORK

FAX TO:

MS CRYSTAL PEAKS
NOTRE DAME HIGH SCHOOL
MALIN BRIDGE
SHEFFIELD

If Sister Frances has not already set
out, we strongly advise that she should
postone her visit until a later date.
Recent falls of snow have made the
hospital drive treacherous to motor
vehicles.

   Dr Pattram is unfortunately unable
to meet Sister Frances this afternoon as
she is preoccupied with assisting
members of the police with their
enquiries concerning a missing patient.

   She would be more than pleased to
arrange a meeting with Sister Frances
at a later date.

Penny Stone

Hospital Secretary

11

'Perhaps he was a workman,' Marie suggests, picking up a pair of eyeball earrings with matching necklace. 'Perhaps he was changing a light bulb or something and then – when the show started – it was too late for him to pop out of the way. He just had to stand there.'

I scrutinise the price tag on a packet of black sugar rats. I think the twins might like them although my mother may not be too pleased. 'You'd think they'd change the light bulbs at night though, wouldn't you? After it had closed.'

Marie has her eye on a life-sized inflatable skeleton. 'I think this'll look dead good in my room.' Fortunately, it does come neatly folded in a discreet, flat packet. Otherwise, I wouldn't feel too happy about it occupying the space next to us on the train going home.

I gaze along the shelves of souvenirs: *Headless Harry* cut-out fun books, tubs of blue, red and yellow slime and packets of skeleton and gravestone stickers. There isn't much I can afford, of course. I've already bought most of my presents and I've got to save some money for the automata museum.

'Perhaps one of the models had fallen over,' Marie suggests again, 'and he'd had to go in and fix it.' She collects together an armful of assorted skeletons, eyeballs and tombstones and begins to head towards the counter. 'Or perhaps the cassette had broken down.'

I stand beside her in the queue. 'I still can't see why he didn't just walk out, though,' I explain. 'I mean,

61

there must be another door. How else did that Asian woman get out?'

Beside us on the counter, there's a display of fudge in blood-red boxes with The York Dungeon inscribed in Gothic black. 'Oh, I'll just have one of these,' adds Marie as the assistant tots up her purchases. 'No, no, you'd better make it two. And . . . just look at these candles.' She selects a tiny spider-encrusted coffin with a skeleton clambering out. 'It'll look really nice on my dressing-table. Isn't he cute? Why don't you get one, Teresa?'

We hook the plastic carriers over our arms and head towards the exit.

'Well, time for a little something,' suggests Marie. 'What do you fancy? Ice cream? Cakes? Pancakes . . . ? Pancakes and cake? Pancakes, cake and ice cream . . . ?'

Our intention had been to find a café with lots of ice-cream sundaes but that was before it turned so cold and began to snow. 'Well, coffee and cream cakes would be nice,' I suggest, 'or pancakes – hot pancakes with fruity fillings and chocolate fudge sauce . . .'

'And ice cream on the top!' adds Marie. 'We've passed lots of nice caffs on the way.'

Our plan is to spend half an hour getting seriously bloated, then go to the automata museum. After that, we're hoping to visit York Minster and the Bar Convent. I'm not all that excited about seeing Margaret Clitherow's severed hand, but we have brought Sister's candle with us and the matches she gave us to light it with.

*

The train now arriving on Platform 5 is the delayed InterCity service from Newcastle. We apologise for the late arrival of this train.

*We would remind passengers that, under the present
inclement weather conditions, all services may be subject
to delay. This is due to snow on the line and heavy
drifting in places. All passenger services are likely to be
affected.*

The staff canteen filled up as drivers and conductors
waited to take out trains that hadn't yet arrived.

'Well, so long as we're all right for gettin' to the pub,'
observed Ken for the umpteenth time.

Les finished off another plate of chips. 'We've got
plenty o' time. Don't worry.'

Ken shook his head. 'I don't know what we're
worryin' about anyway. We've done all right so far.'

'We did all right last time.'

The Jolly Rogers had been sitting smugly in their
usual corner of the bar surrounded by their team of
enthusiastic supporters when Granville had announced,
'Second question for the Flying Scotsmen: Which
famous doctor, played by Tom Baker, became famous
for his fight against the Daleks?'

Les didn't know the names of any famous doctors.
'What about Carter?' he suggested. 'He works in 'ospital.
He should know about doctors.'

'Don't you know, Carter?' Ken had asked.

Carter looked puzzled. 'What was the name of the
actor?' he asked.

Ken called out to the quizmaster: 'Who?'

'That's right!' exclaimed Granville. 'Dr Who. Very
good indeed. Another point for the Flying Scotsmen.'

And a round of applause from the customers in The
Grapes of Wath.

★

'Well, what did you think to the Dungeon, then?' asks

Marie, spooning hot chocolate sauce over her cherry pancake with extra cream.

My brain reels back to the kaleidoscope of severed limbs and rolling heads, blood and intestines, strangled cries, and bodies sliced in half. I cut off a wodge of pancake and dip it in strawberry sauce. 'Gory.'

'Well, I thought it was brilliant,' Marie enthuses, blending together her cherries, chocolate sauce and extra cream. 'I thought the beheading was really good, and The Rack . . . The Rack was good. And Roasting. I liked Roasting. But I think the really best bit was . . .' she pauses, trying to decide.

'It's not a film,' I interrupt. I realize then that that's what I don't like about the Dungeon – the awful realisation that all the exhibits aren't scenes from a film or chapters in a book – they're things that have actually happened. Even the most sickening and gruesome tableaux are depictions of actual things that have happened some time or other to real people. 'It's real. That's what makes it so horrible.'

Marie shakes her head. 'That's what makes it so *good*. If somebody'd made it up, it wouldn't be as gory, would it?'

I ladle a spoonful of sauce across my pancake. 'When people make films and videos, though, they get paid for it. They know it's just for entertainment. These were real people. People being tortured and dying.'

'I know,' gloats Marie, spooning her cream and chocolate sauce together. 'And remember . . .' she waves her chocolate, cherry and sauce-filled spoon right across my face, 'it's all been done in the name of *religion*.'

I wipe the splodge out of my eye with a serviettte.

'And anyway,' she carries on, 'they aren't even real actors in there. They have real people in films. Those are just models. Nothing inside the Dungeon is real at all, is it?'

'What about that man in the Guy Fawkes show?'

'Well, he was a mistake, wasn't he? Some poor man who'd lost his way.' She goes straight into her Sister-Frances-in-Morning-Assembly voice. 'A lost soul. One of those who live lives of fantasy and nightmare. He'll probably be locked up in St Aiden's psychiatric hospital with Agnes this time next week.'

I try to erase from my mind the awful cranking of the rack, the stretching of tortured limbs, and the groans of pain as I concentrate on trying to enjoy my pancake. 'Anyway,' I mutter with my mouth full of cream and strawberry filling, 'what have we done with the map? We need to find our way from here to the automata museum.'

12

It becomes even more difficult to find our way around as the snow deepens and the names on the signposts are secreted in soft, white woolly shrouds. Marie holds tightly to my arm as we slither and slide along the winding streets, our heads bent against the blizzard.

'I thought the main road was supposed to be down here.'

'I thought the Minster was just round the back there.'

'We'll have to look at the map again.'

We shelter inside a shop doorway with a blast of warm air to help our ankles defrost. We turn up our jacket collars and huddle into the corner with our backs against the biting wind. Marie unfolds the map and I reorganise my carriers. The books I bought for the twins are already damp round the edges with snow.

'I think we're just across the river from the station,' suggests Marie.

I bury one carrier inside the other then gaze out of the doorway and scrutinise the sky. It's still as grey and heavy as a well-used floorcloth. There's no sign at all of the snow relenting. 'Do you think . . . ?' I don't like to suggest this, but I really think I ought to say it. 'You don't think the trains might stop, do you?'

'How do you mean?'

'Well, if it carries on snowing . . . I mean, do you think the trains might . . . well, not be able to get through?'

Marie shakes her head dismissively. 'No. 'Course not. They're too big. They're not like cars.'

What I'm really thinking is that it might be sensible, as we're not too far away from the station now, to just go back and check – before the train lines all freeze up and before we freeze to death.

I glance towards what I think is the direction of the railway. 'Don't you think we ought to just go back and make sure?'

Marie raises her eyebrows scornfully.

'If we just checked that the trains were all right then we wouldn't have to worry. We could just carry on round all the museums and things.'

But Marie shows no interest in the suggestion whatsoever. 'And perhaps we ought to ask somebody to see us across the road,' she scoffs. 'Oh no, I forgot, we mustn't talk to any strange men, must we?'

She points out our place on the map again. 'Look. We're here.'

I nod.

'And we want to go there.' Marie rests a frozen finger on the Museum of Automata. 'And there.' She points out the Bar Convent. 'We've got to light Sister's candle, haven't we?'

I nod in resignation as Marie refolds her map and links her arm in mine. 'Come on, then. Are we set?'

We begin to slide together through the snow. We've stopped singing now, saving our energy for breathing and keeping warm. 'Just promise me,' I gasp as the driving snowflakes sting my face, 'that we won't get stuck in York all night. I mean, we can't afford to stay in a hotel.'

'Well, we could always go back to the Dungeon,' Marie suggests. 'We could snuggle up together in that big, roomy cauldron by that nice, hot, roasting fire. Or on the rack. I'm sure there was room for an extra one in there.'

We both chuckle.

'Or in that nice, comfy bed they made for Margaret Clitherow. I'm sure there was room there for two.'

★

'Do you know how long it's taken Darren to get down here from Newcastle?'

Melted snow slid from the sleeves of exhausted train drivers and dripped to the floor of the station canteen.

'Can you put some more chips on, love?'

Chip-greased fingers swirled circles on the steamed-up windows as conductors scrutinised the station platform, searching for overdue trains.

'They say it's six foot deep in Scotland. And it's gettin' worse.'

'Aren't there any more chips?'

'Do you mind just turnin' up the radio, love? We want to listen to the weather.'

Ken rubbed a small patch of steam from the window and peered out as he finished his third mug of tea. 'It's still comin' down pretty heavy,' he told Les. 'It's gonna be chaos if it carries on.'

Les took a large bite of bacon butty. 'Wouldn't be so bad if we'd 'ad any warning. I don't know what they pay them weather forecasters for.'

Ken nodded. 'Well, so long as we're back for tonight.'

'Oh, we'll be back all right,' Ken dipped his butty in the pool of solidifying bacon fat in the centre of his plate. 'We'll be there. If we have to sledge it, we'll be there.' He grinned. 'If we have to ski-jump, we'll be there. In less than five hours time . . .' his eyes sparkled with joyful anticipation, '. . . we'll be winners of the South Yorkshire John Sanella Quiz League. This year's champions, eh? How does that sound?'

Ken grinned.

. . . and here is a snow warning . . .

'Turn the wireless up, love.'

Conversation in the canteen died down as everyone strained their ears to decipher the crackle from the speaker above the chip pan.

Heavy falls of snow are expected throughout most of the region with drifting on high ground. Temperatures are unlikely to rise above freezing and driving conditions will be treacherous. Heavy drifting has caused the closure of many minor roads and police are advising drivers to stay at home this evening.

'Hope them Jolly Rogers are listenin',' added Ken. 'We could do with them staying at 'ome.'

'Well it'd give us a slightly better chance.'

Police say there has been a sighting in York this afternoon of the patient who escaped earlier today from St Aiden's Hospital near York . . .

'That's that place where Carter works, isn't it?' asked Ken. 'You know, that place you pointed out when we were comin' up.'

'That's right. St Aiden's. Hope they're not keepin' Carter in to search the grounds or nothin'. We'll be needin' young Carter tonight.'

A man answering to the description of the missing patient was spotted by two witnesses in the Friargate area but the man had disappeared by the time the police arrived . . .

'You know that bloke who thinks that he's a train?'

'Mmm?'

'Is he that bloke whose father used to drive a 125?' There was a pause. 'Loxley Valley, they called him.'

'Oh yeah?' Les looked up. 'Name rings a bell. Wasn't he the bloke that was involved with that . . .' he hesitated.

69

Ken nodded uncertainly. 'Bonfire Night.'

Police have repeated their warning that this man could be dangerous. Anyone who sees a man answering to his description should contact the police immediately.

13

The Museum of Automata is situated on Tower Street, across the road from Clifford's Tower. We stagger inside, our faces smarting from the driving snow and our ears ablaze from the biting wind. We fumble with numb and swollen fingers to open our purses as melted snow drips from our hair, our jackets, our leggings and our boots, forming icy puddles on the floor.

'You can leave your coats here, if you like,' the ticket lady offers. I don't know whether she's just being kind or trying to avoid spending the rest of the afternoon walking behind us with a mop and bucket.

'Thank you very much.'

'You can leave your parcels here as well. I'll find some newspaper.'

We place our rucksack and carriers on the floor and take off our coats. Marie's thin jacket now has the feel of a soaked and soggy ice-cream wafer.

The ticket lady drapes our coats across a radiator. 'They may not dry completely by the time you're ready to leave,' she warns, 'but at least they'll be nice and warm.'

'That's very kind of you. Thank you very much.'

'I'll put your bags down here and keep an eye on them.' She places a folded newspaper by the side of the ticket desk to soak up the snow from our carriers.

The first room has rows of seats facing a video wall. A notice tells us to sit down and wait for the presentation.

Marie and I use the time to comb the snow out of our hair.

'I'm freezing,' I moan. 'I can't even feel my toes. We could die of hypothermia.'

Marie tries to pat her hair dry with her tissues as the video starts to tell us about clockwork toys and models through the ages and explains about some of the items on display. I take advantage of our seats in the semidarkness to take off my boots and try to massage my feet back into life.

'Perhaps we could find some paper towels,' Marie suggests. 'I've run out of tissues and my hankie's all soaked.'

'They might have some in the loo.'

After the video, I pull my boots back on my swollen feet and start to hobble around the museum.

There are musical boxes and clocks and tiny, trilling, feathered birds. 'It's a shame they're all standing still,' I complain.

'I know. I thought they'd all be wound up and moving round.'

In the first few rooms, the exhibits stand motionless in their glass cases. A beautifully-dressed, porcelain-faced doll pauses in pouring out tea from a miniature teapot; a monkey painting a landscape sits with his brush poised between the picture and his palette; a ruff-collared acrobat balances a cutely-dressed pig on the tip of his ladder. Each of the display areas has a monitor screen showing close-ups of the models working. 'It'd still be better if they wound them all up,' Marie complains.

We walk through to the next gallery which is very different. Everything in here moves. The first exhibit is a seated skeleton wearing a string vest who treadles a sewing machine when we press his footpad.

'Oh, this is good.'

We wander round the room, winding handles and pressing levers and buttons.

'Here. Have a go on this.'

We manipulate the arms on mechanical robots on a machine that tips balls into a chute. 'This is good.'

We play tunes on a funny keyboard.

'Look at that – WELCOME TO THE PIER.'

We walk through the display of jokey, seaside-postcard characters. Cancan dancers swirl their skirts above miniature shoals of fishnet-covered thighs; a drunken man tilts back a bottle of beer and wees into a bucket hidden beneath his seat; another bemused man disappears down the toilet each time we press the button that works the flush.

'These have got no clothes on.'

We giggle at the roundabout of cyclists, the first group dressed in smart Edwardian costume, the second group in their underwear and the third family completely nude.

'There's some toilets there. I'll just see if they've got any paper towels.'

It doesn't seem so important now because we're starting to dry off, but I decide to go to the toilet anyway. When I come out, I walk over to one of the sinks and set the hot tap running. The water's really nice and warm so I spend rather a long time washing my hands. I use a hand-drier on the wall to dry them. I'm just looking round to see if they have any paper towels as well when I realize that the door to one of the cubicles has opened. Of course, I don't turn round and stare to see who it is – I'm a bit more polite than that. I just carry on twisting my hands round in the warm air. There's a mirror above the sinks. I only glance in it. I don't have a proper look because – like most mirrors they have in toilets – it's too

73

high up for me. I can only see the top of my head and down as far as my nose.

So, I just glance up at the mirror and then my mouth falls open. The person who's just walked out of the cubicle – whose reflection I can now see clearly – the person into whose eyes I suddenly find myself staring – is a man. I stand motionless, my fingers halted inside the stream of warm air, like one of the exhibits in the glass cases, poised in mid-motion, paralysed to the spot.

I see myself in the mirror, my eyes open wide and my jaw dropped down. I know I look stupid but, for a couple of seconds, I feel as if I just can't move.

The man in the mirror is very tall and also extremely fat. His hair is cropped short, almost shaved, round his rectangular-shaped head. He has a flabby cushion of double chins where the front of his neck ought to be. There's a row of marks, like an oily necklace, strung along the side of his neck. It might be a line of tattoos.

Of course, I don't have any doubts at all that it's the man we saw standing in the Guy Fawkes tableau. The man who looked so out of place in the torture chamber. The man who moved just as the lights were dimmed.

I don't say anything. I daren't say anything. I just stand for a couple of seconds, stationed between the air-stream and the sink.

The man doesn't wash his hands. He knows I've seen him, though. He gives a little cough as though he's about to say something but then seems to change his mind. Our eyes only meet for a fraction of a second and then he turns and walks towards the door. I watch him leave as I breathe out a sigh of relief. He's wearing a dark jacket and trousers, and a pair of black Doc Martens boots. He's carrying something red rolled in a bundle underneath his arm.

'He must be some sort of workman. He must be fixing things in all the different museums.'

'But why would he? He didn't have a toolbox or anything. What could he be mending?'

'He might be an inspector. Checking on safety or things to do with fire regulations.'

We're standing in the French Gallery where the monitors now display a completely different sequence of musicians, performing animals and acrobats. I watch a banjo player wearing a straw boater and bow tie. Inside the glass case, he stands lifelike but motionless; on the screen, he turns his head, moves his shoulders and opens and closes his eyelids.

'Don't you think we ought to tell somebody? I mean, he could be dangerous.' I lower my voice. 'He might be a child molester.'

Marie gazes at the acrobats – one balancing on one hand on top of a ladder, another balancing a pig. 'He didn't know you were going into the toilets, though, did he? I mean, he went in there before you did.'

That's true.

'So he didn't go in there to . . . to get you.'

I know that what Marie says is right, but I also know that the man looked very suspicious. He didn't look as though he was mending anything or checking on the fire regulations. 'I still think we ought to tell somebody.'

On the screen in front of me, I watch the acrobat and his tiny, cutely-dressed pig. The acrobat's face is painted; his waistcoat is embroidered with sequins and silver thread; the piglet wears a checked shirt and satin waistcoat. The pig grins stupidly as he balances his trotter on the very top of the ladder.

'Perhaps we ought to tell the lady at the cash desk.'

Marie nods.

I turn away from the monitor and notice that my heart is thumping pit-a-pat. I feel hot and sweaty even though I've only just thawed out. I turn and glance over my shoulder. There's no one there. I gaze towards the open doorway. There's nobody about. I still feel shaky, though. I glance around all the exhibits but they just stand motionless inside their glass cases, staring, smiling. Stopped.

I had been looking forward to going round and watching the videos of all the different acrobats and things, but now something about the room has changed. The dolls and acrobats have lost their friendly features. Their tight, fixed grins are more sinister. Their painted faces stare malevolently.

When I was little, we used to play a party game called What's the time, Mr Wolf? We had to creep up behind the person who was the wolf and, when he or she turned around, we had to stand completely still. If they saw us moving, we were out. That's what all the mechanical figures look like now. Something that's sneaked up behind us, waiting their moment to pounce.

'Well,' says Marie, 'Perhaps we ought to go and find the souvenir shop. We seem to be the only people left in the museum.'

14

The shop lady nods sympathetically. 'Well, I'm sorry if you were upset,' she tells me, 'but I suppose . . . I did just lock the door to the Gents, you see. I thought you were the only people left.'

'Oh.'

Marie shoots an 'I told you so' expression across the counter. She still seems to think I should accept any remotely plausible explanation for a refugee from The Gunpowder Plot appearing in the Ladies.

'I was thinking of going home early, you see. What with the weather . . .'

That's presumably why she's already wearing her hat and coat, and has her handbag over her arm and a bunch of keys in her hand.

'Oh look, there's cardboard acrobats you can make yourself,' exclaims Marie. 'They look good.'

The shop lady glances at her watch. I've got a feeling that she isn't all that desperate to serve us.

'Were you just closing?'

'Well . . .' she hesitates. 'If there's anything you particularly want . . .'

'And look at these musical boxes.' Marie picks one up. 'Aren't they gorgeous?'

'I don't want to rush you, but I'm a bit worried that the buses might stop soon. I live quite a long way out you see. And I don't know about the trains . . .'

I glance outside where heavy flakes of snow are still floating, thick and fast. What if the trains have stopped? I feel a sense of rising panic. I did warn Marie . . .

'There's some postcards here with the acrobat on – that one with that little piglet on his ladder.'

'Do you think . . .' I hardly dare to ask. 'Do you think the trains might have stopped already, then?'

'Trains? Oh, I don't know.' The shop lady puts down her bag. 'There was something on the news. I think it said they were delayed. That's right. I don't know if it said there were any cancelled.'

Marie's still examining the musical boxes. I walk across and give her a pat on the shoulder. 'We'd better hurry up,' I whisper. Of course, I've hardly any money left. The musical boxes look very nice but they're much more than I can afford. 'I'll get the coats.'

I walk across to the ticket box and pick up my coat from the radiator. It's still damp on the outside although the lining's warm and dry. I put it on and fasten the zip. One advantage of buying a jacket as thin as Marie's, I realise, is that hers has dried completely. I carry it with our plastic bags and the rucksack back into the souvenir shop.

'It doesn't matter if you want something special,' the lady is explaining, 'but I have actually cashed up now.'

'Come on.' I hold out Marie's coat.

'We'll just work out the way to the convent then. Let's have a look at the map.'

I hold the carriers while Marie takes out the map. My bag seems very light. I look inside and check out the tiny candle I bought from the Dungeon and the post cards and the stickers, but where are my Thomas the Tank Engine books?'

'My books have gone.'

'What books?

'Thomas the Tank Engine. Those activity books – don't you remember?'

78

Marie peers into the bag.

'And the story books. I bought the story books for the twins.'

'Perhaps you left them on the counter.'

I think back. I remember buying the books. And then I remember taking them out of the carrrier while we sheltered in the shop doorway. 'No, I definitely picked them up. I put everything together inside both bags when we stopped to look at the map.'

'Perhaps you dropped them.'

I take a deep breath. Marie can be really exasperating sometimes. How could I have dropped four books without noticing?

'Perhaps they've fallen behind the radiator.'

I don't think that's very likely, but I walk back to the ticket desk while Marie puts on her jacket. I search underneath the radiator, on the shelf and on the counter. I just can't understand it. The rest of my things are still there. If there were thieves about, why didn't they just pick up my bag and walk off with it? Why should it only be the Thomas the Tank Engine books that have vanished into thin air.

'Well, I'm ever so sorry,' says the shop lady. 'I can't think what must have happened.' She takes her keys and unlocks the cupboard underneath the till, but it only has piles of pens and receipt books and spare till rolls. 'Jean had to close up and leave early,' she explains. 'They were sending her children home from school because of the snow.'

'Well, she won't have taken the Thomas the Tank Engine books, will she?' asked Marie.

Might she have stolen them to take home for her children? It doesn't really seem very likely. She seemed such a nice person.

'What about leaving your name and address? Then, if they do turn up, we can send them on.'

I write my name and address on a piece of paper. I try not to look too upset because it's obviously not the shop lady's fault, but I do have a bit of a lump in my throat. I've only just recovered from my ordeal in the ladies' loo. And I'm not used to people stealing from me.

'The twins won't mind, will they?' says Marie. 'Not when you explain.'

'It's not the same though, is it?'

Marie tries to look sympathetic but, of course, she has lots of money. She doesn't understand what it's like to lose something you've had to save up for.

The shop lady glances at the address I've written on her notepad. 'You weren't thinking of going all the way back to Sheffield this afternoon, were you?'

I nod. There seems something slightly ominous about the way she's using the past tense.

'Well,' she says,' looking a bit concerned, 'if you don't mind my saying so, I really think – if you've got nothing else urgent to do – with the weather being like it is – it might be best to start making your way back to the station.'

★

ST AIDEN'S HOSPITAL
NEAR YORK

FAX TO:

MS CRYSTAL PEAKS
NOTRE DAME SCHOOL
MALIN BRIDGE
SHEFFIELD

Sister Frances has asked us to inform you
that she is likely to be late arriving back at
school this afternoon. As she's had problems
with her car, she will now be travelling back
by train.

   Sister suspects that, as most rail services
are being delayed, she will not return in time
for this evening's staff meeting and recom-
mends that it be postponed so that other staff
will not be further inconvenienced. She gives
permission for all staff and pupils to leave
half an hour earlier today.

Best wishes,

Penny Stone

Hospital Secretary
p.p. Myrtle Springs, Chair of Hospital
Management Board

15

'I always maintained that this patient was far too dangerous to be a resident at St Aiden's,' Myrtle Springs complained, as she poured herself another gin and tonic. 'He should have been transferred to one of those special hospitals for the criminally insane.'

'Don isn't actually a criminal, though, Ms Springs,' Carter interrupted. 'He hasn't actually been convicted of any offence.'

Myrtle glowered at Carter as she glugged her gin and tonic. 'Well, don't worry, Nurse Knowle,' she said, scanning the report that she'd prepared for the local police, 'we'll see to that; he soon will be.'

She glanced towards Sumitra, stirring more sugar into her cup of tea. 'If you need to take more time off work, Dr Pattram, we will understand, but . . .' she hesitated, '. . . it won't be too easy for us to find someone else to, er . . . given the . . .'

'I'm quite all right. Really.'

Carter took a deep breath. 'But Dr Pattram's only been off work for a few hours,' he argued. 'It must have been very traumatic for her. I mean, don't you think she ought to take the rest of the week off?'

Myrtle tightened her grip round her glass of gin. 'I always say the best way to get over any personal difficulties is to throw oneself into one's work.'

'Well,' Sumitra took a long drink of her tea, 'I don't actually have any physical injuries.'

'You see, I think it's important to make it clear,' Carter explained, 'that Don did go to some lengths to make sure that no one was actually hurt. I mean, I know it's all been very traumatic for Dr Pattram, but all Don wanted was to take the keys so he could borrow someone's car and . . .'

Myrtle shuddered as she remembered her brand-new car, only recently resprayed after its encounter with the wheelie bin. 'I suppose the carpets will be filthy,' she muttered, 'covered in muddy footprints.'

'Sorry?'

'I always keep a pair of slippers in the car for inclement weather, don't you?' she asked Dr Pattram. 'I hate to drive with a dirty carpet.'

Su said nothing.

'You see, if you don't mind my saying so,' Carter interrupted, 'I don't think it's very helpful for us to keep thinking of Don as a criminal . . .'

Myrtle gritted her teeth before downing the rest of her gin. 'Actually, we've got a little job for you, Nurse Knowle, if you don't mind . . .' She lifted a corner of her heavy velvet curtains and peered outside to where the snowflakes were floating thickly past the window. 'You know Sister Frances – the nun who visits Agnes every week . . . ?'

Carter nodded.

'Apparently her car won't start.'

'Do you want me to give her a push?'

'No, no,' Myrtle sighed. 'I thought you might give her a lift down to the station.'

Carter glanced out at the snow-covered drive. His hopes of getting back home in time for the finals of the John Sanella quiz had been lessening every minute. And of course, he didn't even own a car. He couldn't afford one on the meagre wages he got paid from the hospital. 'I don't really see how I . . .'

Myrtle peered through the double-glazed bay window to where the St Aiden's League of Friends Smile-Away minibus was almost completely covered in snow. 'You can take her in the patients' special minibus if you like.'

★

As soon as we arrive at the station we know there's something wrong.

Outside, beside the taxi rank, a tired, dejected queue coils around the pillars. I think about making some remark about people waiting for the conga to start, but I seem to have no energy left for cracking jokes. We have had a great day out in York, but all I want now is to find a warm, dry train and sit in a comfy seat, knowing that we're safely on our way back home.

We squeeze past the queue into the station concourse, which looks like the entrance to a football ground at ten to three on a Saturday afternoon. Except that nobody is moving. Everyone stands still, staring upwards at the huge display boards which show you the times of the trains.

Wet, forlorn bodies drip melted snow into a lake of slush. Most people look as though they're trying to get home from work. There are also groups of pupils in school uniform, old-aged pensioners looking tired and confused, and parents rocking wailing babies – everyone standing with their heads tilted back, gazing at the long list of TRAIN DELAYED notices.

'Oh no,' groans Marie. 'Why didn't we come back earlier?'

I open my mouth and then close it again.

'Perhaps we could get a cup of tea.'

I've already noticed the long queue snaking out through the doors of the buffet. There's another line of people outside the kiosk that sells crisps and chocolate so I still say nothing. I scrutinise the list of destinations on the board but there's no mention of Sheffield. 'Excuse me,' I ask a harassed-looking railway official squeezing past, 'can you tell us what time there'll be a train to Sheffield?'

To my surprise, the man just points towards the stairs on our right. 'Platform 7,' he explains. 'There's the InterCity through from Newcastle.' He checks his watch 'You'll have to hurry up, though. It's due out any minute.'

'Come on.' I grab Marie's arm as we make a dash. We sidestep round a crying baby muffled inside its buggy; we negotiate a luggage trolley; we clamber up the iron staircase then pound across the wooden bridge.

'There. Bet that's it.'

There'a a train on Platform 7. Even from the wooden bridge I can see it's crammed with passengers. But, as we turn the corner to clatter down the steps, a whistle blows.

'Wait for us!' shouts Marie.

We spring to the bottom of the steps but, just at that moment, the train starts pulling out.

'Come on. We can still catch it.'

We run towards the edge of the platform and I reach for a door handle. The train begins to pick up speed.

'Stop! Sorry. You're too late.' The guard rushes forward and holds out his arm just in time to stop us breaking our necks. 'Stand back.'

We both screech to a halt, standing open-mouthed with disappointment as the train slithers past, crammed tight with passengers. 'Oh, no!'

We wait and watch, panting, getting our breath back as the train glides away like a silver eel along the great curve of track. As it picks up speed, we see the crammed faces at the windows blur into an egg-like mass.

'Well, it did look a bit full.'

'I'd still rather be standing squashed in there than shivering on the platform,' complains Marie.

'Well, perhaps there'll be another one.'

'Where are you going?' asks the guard.

'Sheffield.'

He grins at us. 'Well, you're in luck. There is actually another train for Sheffield over on Platform 2. It's the slow train, I'm afraid. That's why everybody else has got on this, but . . .' he checks his watch. 'It ought to be leaving in a couple of minutes time.'

'Well, at least we can get a seat.' Marie flops down at a table by the window.

'We'd have had to stand all the way on that other one.'

I undo my jacket but don't actually take it off. We're still both shivering with cold. 'Let's hope they put some heating on. It doesn't seem very warm.'

We sit down facing each other as the carriage fills up with passengers. There's a group of schoolgirls, younger than us, wearing neat little uniforms and hats. There are several men wearing overcoats, suits and ties and carrying briefcases. There's a group of younger men wearing dirty overalls.

This is the delayed 16.50 service to Sheffield. Calling at Pontefract, Moorthorpe, Swinton, Rotherham Central, Meadowhall and Sheffield.

'Did you check whether there's a buffet?' asks Marie. 'I wouldn't mind a cup of tea and some nice cake.'

I gaze out of the window at the snow, piled deeply at the side of the track. 'I wouldn't mind several cups of tea, a sausage roll, some iced carrot cake and a few chocolate biscuits,' I answer wistfully, 'but I've a feeling that we might be disappointed.'

'Well, never mind,' says Marie, taking out one of her boxes of Dungeon fudge. 'It won't be long now before we're home.'

16

Les Carr eased the 16.50 to Sheffield out of York station exactly one hour late.

The signals were at green, all systems go, but as Les nosed his locomotive forward, he was aware of the mounting piles of fresh snow bedded beside the track. He'd be lucky to reach Sheffield, he thought, without several unscheduled stops along the way.

Les began to replan his timetable. The quiz started at half past eight. It normally took him over half an hour to drive to the pub from home. With the snow, he'd have to allow at least forty-five minutes. Maybe more. That meant leaving home at seven-thirty at the latest. Half an hour minimum to go home and have something to eat – although if he was late, he could go straight to the pub after he clocked off. Hadn't Ken said something about a chip shop? That'd do nicely. A fish 'n' chip supper would be fine.

The Flying Scotsmen had been rather worried about their chances in the semifinal. Especially after the Jolly Rogers had successfully answered questions on golf, tennis, ancient history and gourmet food.

'We'd do all right if they 'ad a few questions on darts,' suggested Ken.

'Or dominoes,' said Les.

'Or if they had questions on different kinds of beer,' offered Carter.

'Right,' said Granville, 'an arboreal question for the Flying Scotsmen . . .'

Ken, Les and Carter stared at each other with some confusion. 'What's *arboreal*?' asked Carter.

Ken shook his head.

'It'll be something to do with ships 'n' 'arbours,' suggested Les.

'Can anyone tell me the name we give to the colour of someone's eyes when they're a mixture of green and brown?'

Les bit his bottom lip thoughtfully.

Carter frowned.

'A word which is also the name of a tree.'

Ken looked blankly at Les and Les looked blankly at Ken and both of them looked even more blankly at Carter.

'Excuse me.' Ken's wife, Hazel, squeezed past on her way to the bar.

Ken's face lit up. 'It's . . .'

Les and Carter leant forward, eager to catch his words. 'It's what?'

'. . . time we had another drink,' suggested Ken. He called out to his wife now queuing at the bar. 'Hazel!'

'Excellent!' shouted Granville. 'Hazel is another name for a mixture of the colours green and brown. Another point for the Flying Scotsmen.'

And a round of applause from the regulars.

The snow was still falling thick and fast and visibility was poor. Les managed to maintain his speed for the first few miles out of York, but after that the flurries of snow became thicker. He eased his hand off the throttle, reached across and began to twiddle the dials on his old-fashioned radio, hoping to find the weather forecast:

Police have warned motorists to be on the look-out for the dangerous mental patient who escaped this afternoon from the high-security wing of a hospital near York.

The patient overpowered a doctor in her office at the hospital and tied her to a chair. A police spokesperson says that the doctor has not been harmed but is still suffering from shock.

A man answering to the description of the missing patient was given a lift by a middle-aged couple travelling out of York this evening . . .

Les turned up the volume as the woman gave her account:

'*My husband stopped to pick him up because he didn't have a coat on or anything and it was coming down so heavy with the snow. All his clothes were soaked.*'

'*Did you talk to the man?*' asked the reporter.

'*No. Not really, hardly at all. We asked him a few questions but he didn't have much to say for himself.*'

Les edged his way through the banks of snow on the approach to Sherburn station. Visibility wasn't getting any better.

'*Can you remember what he looked like?*'

'*He was very tall. Very big with short hair. He had like a double chin. He was wearing jeans and some black boots – and I did notice this row of tattoos all round his neck. I thought it was a bruise at first.*'

'*And where did you take him to?*'

'*Well, he said he was going to the station. We set him down next to the railway line – near to Moorthorpe. He said he was going to catch a train.*'

Les noticed a small red light visible in the distance. He began to ease on the brakes.

It looked as if the signals were at red.

*

'We wondered if the snack trolley would be arriving

soon?' Marie asks the conductor as she offers him our tickets.

The conductor is a small man with a very large tummy and a long beaked nose. As he carefully checks the details on our tickets, Marie mouths silently to me, Penguin.

It's the dark-coloured jacket and white shirt that make him look as though he ought to be waddling along on an ice floe with a fish hanging out of his beak. I stifle a giggle but the man says nothing.

'We haven't been able to find the buffet car.'

The penguin takes a deep breath. 'There is no buffet car,' he tells us through his slightly gritted beak. 'And no snack trolley. In fact, you're very lucky to have found a train.' He passes back our tickets. 'And even more lucky to have found a train that's moving.'

But Marie doesn't sound particularly grateful. 'We didn't get anything to eat on the station.'

'Well, nor did I.' He shakes his head. 'The canteen had completely run out of chips by the time we got there. They'd had no deliveries all afternoon. Just think yourself lucky – I haven't eaten since breakfast.'

Marie holds out her packet of Dungeon fudge. 'Well, would you care for a piece of fudge?'

The conductor reaches out his hand, then hesitates. 'It's the last one.'

'Well, that's all right. We wouldn't want you to starve to death.'

The train doesn't stay moving for long. It slows right down, then pauses, then starts again, even slower. It eventually grinds to a complete halt.

'Where are we?' I gaze out of the window but all I can see is darkness. Dense, oppressive blackness lightened only by white splodges thudding against the carriage window.

'I don't know.' Marie rubs her hand in a circle on the glass but it doesn't improve the view. 'I can't see a station.'

'Well, I hope we haven't broken down.'

'I don't fancy getting out to push.'

'I'll tell you what we can do.' Marie lifts her rucksack on to the table and takes out her notebook and pen. 'We'll start our project on Margaret Clitherow. That'll give us something exciting to think about.'

'It might be more exciting to climb outside and push the train.'

Marie grins. 'Come on.' She unscrews the top from her pen and writes the heading:

THE MARGARET CLITHEROW EXPERIENCE

'Now, the way I imagine it to be,' she explains, turning the page round so I can see it, 'is a *hands-on* experience.'

'How do you mean?'

'Well, instead of just writing out the story of Margaret Clitherow – because that would be a bit boring – we make this sort of a game.'

'We can't make a game about a Catholic martyr being squashed to death with rocks.'

Marie nods enthusiastically. 'Yes, we can. It doesn't have to be silly. It can be a serious game; it'll be a game to work out who was responsible for Margaret's death. That's what Sister asked us, isn't it?'

'Mmm.'

'So I suggest we think of all the different characters involved and we give them all a certain number of points depending on how much they were to blame.'

'How do we decide?'

Marie doesn't look too sure. 'We'll come to that later. Then, I'll tell you what . . .' She screws up a piece of fudge wrapper to make a tiny ball, then bends part of the empty fudge box to make a sort of chute. '. . . we make some tiny miniature rocks and we tip them down this chute.'

I start to giggle.

'At the bottom there'll be a model of Margaret Clitherow – made out of paper or straw or something – and we see how many rocks it'll take to squash her flat.'

I don't see how we could possibly hand this in for our project, but it'll give us something to do, especially as the train's still not started. 'Go on, then. We could make a sort of board game, couldn't we?'

'That's right. We'll have cards with the names on of all the different characters. There'll be different squares you land on where you have to pick up a character card.'

'All right then. Let's make a list.' I take out a pen and write:

Characters responsible for Margaret's death

17

Les Carr checked his watch. Thirty minutes late so far which, added to the time lost in York station, made one hour thirty minutes. He'd already decided that he wouldn't have time to go home and get washed and changed before setting out for the pub – he'd be better heading straight there from the station. The important thing was not to lose any more time. He stared at the red signal in front of him, willing it to change. Keep calm, Les, he told himself. No use gettin' all worked up.

The fact that they were in the final at all seemed like a miracle. They'd never expected to make it through the first few rounds of the quiz. However, the Flying Scotsmen had – against everybody's expectations – stormed through the semifinal with flying colours.

Carter's moment of glory had arrived when Granville had asked: 'Can anyone tell me the name of the man who invented the steam engine?'

Ken shook his head at Les and Les shook his head at Ken and both of them gazed expectantly at Carter.

Carter looked very puzzled. 'What?' he asked.

'James Watt. Very good indeed!' announced Granville. 'The inventor of the steam engine and another point for the Flying Scotsmen.'

The team were still congratulating each other when Granville started his next question. 'Going on from that,' he asked, 'can anyone tell me the nationality of James Watt?'

'I thought it was . . .' Carter started.

'What?' Ken and Les leant forward eagerly.

'. . . about time for another drink,' said Carter.

By this time, Ken's wife, Hazel, had reached the front of the queue at the bar. 'Can I get you anything?' she called across to Ken.

It was actually Ken's turn to buy the drinks, but he decided to let Hazel buy him a whisky to be going on with. 'Scotch!' he called across.

'Very good!' Granville announced. 'The nationality of James Watt was Scots or Scottish. And with that, ladies and gentlemen, the Flying Scotsmen take the lead.'

And another round of applause from the regulars.

*

Ladies and gentlemen, we shall shortly be arriving at Pontefract station. All passengers for Pontefract.

The party of schoolgirls wearing their neat brown uniforms start to rub their eyes and sit up.

We do apologise for the late arrival of this train.

Businessmen begin to button up their overcoats and pick up their brollies.

'Good gracious! We're actually arriving at a station,' Marie announces with exaggerated enthusiasm. 'And it's only taken us . . . what . . . ?' She looks at her watch, 'An hour and ten minutes.'

'It would have been quicker to walk.'

'Or ski.'

'Or we could have easily got here by sledge.'

We both stare out of the window, eager for the change of scenery. 'Well, if we're coming to a station,' suggests Marie, 'I wonder if there's anywhere we could buy something to eat.'

I scour the blackness outside for the slightest sign of a station shop or café. 'It'd be nice if they had a snack bar. Just think – piping hot soup and chips and burgers.'

'Or what about coffee and chocolate fudge cake with hot chocolate fudge sauce?'

'Or some of that ginger cake with icing on the top.'

'Or even a bar of chocolate.'

The train grinds to a halt. There's a steady stream of embarking passengers buttoned against the blizzard: business men, workmen in their overalls and donkey jackets, schoolchildren . . . but no sign of a snack bar.

'It's like one of those places on the miniature railway.'

'What do you mean?' asks Marie.

'Small. Much too small to have a shop or a café or anything.' I sigh. 'And anyway, we mustn't get off the train. We wouldn't want it to go without us.'

'Well, the speed we've been travelling,' scoffs Marie, 'we could easily run after it and catch it up.'

I gaze out of the window as the banks of cushioned snow glisten in the station lights. 'There's hardly anybody waiting.'

'They've probably decided to walk instead. Anyway, I suppose most of the people going to Sheffield will have caught that earlier train.'

'I wonder if that one had a buffet.'

I do notice one figure down towards the other end of the platform. She's wearing a long black skirt, black boots, black flowing headgear and a familiar white circle round her face. 'There's a nun.'

'Better not be Sister Frances,' Marie shrieks in horror. She crosses her fingers into a crucifix and holds it against the glass. 'Can you see any warts?'

'Not from here.'

'Has she got a hooked nose?'

'Can't quite tell.'

Marie presses her palms together piously in front of her face. 'Dear Lord, please guide our dear Sister to a different compartment of this train. We don't mind where she sits but keep her away from us.'

'I think your prayer's worked,' I giggle. 'She's getting on further down.'

This is the delayed 18.30 train to Sheffield. Calling at Moorthorpe, Doncaster, Rotherham Central, Meadowhall and Rotherham . . .

'Anyway,' I reassure Marie, as the doors close and the train starts inching forward, 'Sister said she was doing something important at school today. Don't you remember?'

Marie nods. 'Interviews. That was why she couldn't go and visit Agnes.' She glances towards the door in between the compartments. 'It'd better not be her anyway. We're not exactly wearing our school uniform.'

'And we never lit the candle.'

Marie nods. 'But the convent *was* closed. I mean, we have got an excuse.'

I sigh. 'Well, Sister might have been expecting us to go there first . . .'

'But anyway,' Marie wags her finger at me, 'we are working very hard on our project.' She holds up the piece of file paper. 'I think we're doing very well indeed.

Characters responsible for Margaret's death

- *The man with the rocks who was actually paid to kill her.*
- *Judge Rhodes who passed sentence.*
- *The young boy who revealed Margaret's hiding place.*
- *The constable who arrested her.*
- *Queen Elizabeth I who made it illegal to be a catholic.*
- *Henry May – Margaret's stepfather???? (Was he Lord Major?)*
- *Edwin Sandys – the Archbishop of York who hated Catholics.*
- *The Earl of Huntingdon (president of York Council in 1572 who was determined to eliminate catholics from the city.)*
- *Margaret's husband (could he have helped to save her? Did he want to get rid of her?)*
- *The Earl of Northumberland.*
- *The judge who ordered Northumberland's head to be spiked on the wall. Margaret herself – for refusing to be tried by anyone but God. (Peine forte et dure – pressing to death was the penalty for refusing to plead in court.)*

18

'He'll be here soon enough, don't worry,' Ken insisted as Carter lifted a corner of the curtains and peered out into the pub car park.

Carter could see soft snow sparkling on rooftops, chimneypots and telephone wires; he could see snow glistening under the lights of the chip shop at the end of the street; he could see a snowman standing beside the hospital's Smile-Away minibus. But he couldn't see any sign of Les.

'Another beer?' Ken motioned towards Carter's glass.

'I'm all right for now, thanks.'

'We'll just wait till he gets here, then.'

The Jolly Rogers and their party of supporters were lounging at the opposite side of the bar. 'Do we think we need another crate?' someone asked.

'Well, it won't be wasted, will it?' They were already surrounded by several crates of beer, bottles of wine and champagne.

'Looks as though they're expecting to have something to celebrate,' Ken observed.

Carter nodded. 'Well, they might if Les doesn't turn up.'

'He'll turn up all right.'

'We'll be no good with just two of us.'

Ken and Carter sat isolated in their corner as another flotilla of Jolly Rogers supporters floated into the pub. '*Here we go, here we go, here we go!*' they sang, shaking snow on to the polished boards.

'Did you say you'd driven here in a minibus?' asked Ken.

'That's right,' Carter drank down his beer. 'I had to give this woman – a nun, she was – a lift down to the station. I was supposed to go off duty at two o'clock.' He shook his head. 'They won't exactly miss that minibus. They've got no plans to take the patients anywhere – not in this weather.'

'I wondered whether you might not get here,' Ken confided, 'when I 'eard about that lad escapin'. I thought you might have got set on lookin' for 'im.'

Carter nodded. 'Well, we were searching all morning till we found out he'd taken somebody's car. Then it was handed over to the police.'

Ken took a long swig of his beer. 'It said on the news he was dangerous. Has he killed somebody, or what?'

Carter picked up a soggy beer mat and began folding it between his fingers. 'Well, personally, I don't think he's dangerous at all, but everybody else seems to. He has got a bit of a thing about trains, but . . .'

'What do they call him?'

'Don. Donald Valley.'

Ken frowned.

'Why?'

'It's just that . . . well, I used to know his dad, you know. Loxley.'

Carter looked up at Ken with sudden interest. 'Really? You knew Donald's dad?'

'Used to drive an InterCity.'

Carter drained the last drops from his glass. 'Do you know anything about Don then? How he got . . . you know . . . how he finished up . . . ?'

Ken nodded sagely. 'Oh, I can tell you all about that. All about the train crash. Bonfire Night. I can tell you all about it.'

100

Carter picked up Ken's glass. 'I'd better get you another pint in, then.'

★

'Another one at red.'

Les Carr gritted his teeth as yet another red signal loomed out of the darkness, a tiny, bloodshot eye on the horizon. He'd only just set off from the last long stop but now he grudgingly began to ease on the brake again.

'It's not gettin' any better.'

Les could actually see for himself that it wasn't getting any better. Orgreave, however – Orgreave was his senior conductor – hadn't been able to stop telling him that it wasn't getting any better every two or three minutes since he came to stand in the cab. Les had been able to see that it wasn't getting any better for the last hour and a half. He was beginning to think that, if Orgreave told him once more that it wasn't getting any better, he'd be tempted to open the door of the cab, kick him out into the snow and hope he never got better at all.

Les glanced at his watch with the time coming up to ten past eight. A prospect for salvation had been forming in his mind. If the signal changed and they managed to keep moving, in another ten or fifteen minutes their train would actually be passing the Railway Tavern where the quiz would be just about to start.

'How many passengers did you say there were?'

'Not many. Nearly everybody for Sheffield must have got that earlier train out of York.'

Les nodded sagely. 'I'm thinkin' of leavin' you in charge for a minute when we get to Moorthorpe. I might get out an' use the phone. They'll probably have one in that pub.'

Orgreave nodded.

'I'll phone the signals. See what the situation's like further down. They might well tell us to transfer 'em all at Doncaster.'

Orgreave began to wonder about the possibility of food being served in the pub although they probably wouldn't have anything much at that time of night. 'Sounds like a good idea. You could get us both a packet of crisps – or some of those pork scratchings.'

Les opened his mouth to tell Orgreave that there was actually a fish and chip shop down the road, not too far from the Railway Tavern. Then he changed his mind. He needed to leave someone in charge of the train.

★

The clock above the bar said eight twenty-five. Ken had thought about phoning Les at home but he knew there was no point. Les would be doing his level best to get to the Railway Tavern, he was certain of that.

Ken stood in the queue at the bar amidst the crowd of Jolly Rogers supporters.

'Should be a good do tonight.'

'Apparently they've hired a karaoke.'

Their only other hope would be to recruit another team member, but as Ken looked round the bar, he realised that all the regulars in the Railway Tavern seemed to be rooting for the Jolly Rogers. Most importantly, everyone seemed to have been invited to the celebration party afterwards.

'Everything all right?' Granville, the quizmaster, appeared at Ken's side.

'Well, we're still one man short. I was wondering if somebody else might like to . . .'

He gazed at the crowd around the bar, many of them

102

sporting skull and crossbones sweatshirts, badges and scarves.

'You'll have a job,' Granville warned. 'All the regulars have been invited to the party. They won't want to be seen associatin' with you lot.'

Ken nodded. 'Two pints of bitter, please,' he asked the barmaid.

He was elbowed out of the way by a very large figure at the bar. He turned round and saw an Asian woman wearing a red silk sari. 'Good evening,' he said.

The woman nodded but said nothing.

19

'I wonder if we're nearly there.' Marie rubs her finger on the window and peeps out into the blackness.

I don't even bother trying to look out. 'We can't be. We've only passed one station.' Marie must know as well as I do that there's at least five stations in between York and Sheffield. That means we've actually only completed about one fifth of the journey.

'I thought that might be Meadowhall over there.'

I don't reply. I wrap my jacket as tightly as I can round my shoulders and concentrate on our list of Clitherow-game characters. 'I think the man who piled the rocks on should have most points,' I explain, 'because he was the person who actually killed her.'

Marie glances back at the list. 'Well, I think he should score the least.'

'Why?'

'Because he was just a beggar standing outside in the street. If he didn't want the job of killing her, they'd have just found somebody else.'

I think about that for a moment. 'But he still did it.'

The train slows down yet again. I clench my teeth and hiss slightly but manage to say nothing.

'He might have had a wife and children at home and they might have been starving to death.' Marie massages her hands together. 'His family might have been freezing and he might have needed that money for firewood and a bowl of stew and . . .' she gazes wistfully out of the window again, '. . . a bag of hot chips and some steaming meat pies and a piping hot Cornish pasty.' She screws her thin jacket cuffs derisively in her hands. 'Or some nice, big, woolly jumpers.'

The train stops again. 'Oh no.' I can hardly believe it. 'We're never going to get home.'

Marie breathes on the window and rubs a bigger circle so that she can peer out. 'Well, I've got some exciting news for you, Teresa.'

'What's that?'

'We've actually reached *another* station.'

I take a deep breath. 'Are you sure? They haven't announced anything.'

'Here. Have a look.'

I lean forward and peer out of the cleared circle of glass. I can just make out a long, low building snuggled in snow. 'It looks like one of those stables like they have in nativity scenes.'

'You mean there's a load of animals and shepherds waiting for the train.'

'No. Don't be stupid.'

'And three wise men – and a star. And a little crib with a . . .'

'I just mean it's covered in snow.'

'Good gracious me!' exclaims Marie in mock amazement. 'Snow? Oh, I am surprised.'

The snow on the platform is like a heavy cotton duvet, completely unblemished, without a single footprint. 'I can't see anyone about.'

Marie peers out too. 'Well, what have we stopped for, then?'

No one's climbing off the train and there's no one waiting to climb on. I can't see the name of the station anywhere but I can see a building with lights.

'There's somebody over there, look.' Marie points

towards the engine. A small dark figure is just clambering out of the cab. 'It must be the driver.'

'What a cheek! Where does he think he's going?'

'Perhaps he's going to fetch the buffet trolley.' Marie's face brightens.

'They'll have to put it on skis.'

'Or he could pull it on a sledge.'

'Perhaps he's going to find somebody to fix the heating.'

We both watch as the black, huddled figure trudges through the snow and into the station.

'Well,' Marie gives a long, drawn-out sigh, 'I hate to say this Teresa, but I do hope he's not decided to set off home and leave us stranded here all night.'

*

'I don't know if you might be any good at Geography,' Ken suggested to the Asian woman standing at the bar. 'That's one of our weak spots. That an' . . .' he thought for a moment, '. . . well, History an' Sport an' Music an' all that sort o' stuff.'

The Asian woman nodded understandingly as she drank her pint of bitter.

'Les must have got held up,' Ken told her as he paid for his two pints of beer. 'We were expecting 'im half an hour ago. He's been driving a train down from York.'

The Asian woman cocked her head slightly as though she were starting to take an interest.

'I think he must have 'ad a few problems with the weather. Anyway,' Ken picked up his two pint glasses, 'if you think you'd like to join the team, we'd be more than pleased to have you.' When there was no reply, he added, 'I could get you a pint in if you like . . .'

But at that very moment, the door to the Railway Tavern burst open.

"'Ang on,' shouted Ken as Les himself dashed across towards the bar. 'What time do you call this then, eh?'

'What a journey! What a night!'

'Well, I'm certainly glad to see you.' Ken helped Les off with his snow-covered coat. 'How've you got here, then?'

'On a bloomin' train,' chuckled Les. 'How else? I've parked it across the road.'

He slammed a large bunch of keys down on the bar while he took some change out of his pocket. 'I'll have a mug of coffee, please,' he asked the barmaid. 'I'm still on duty, officially,' he explained to Ken.

'Well, we're certainly glad to see you, anyhow,' said Ken. 'I was just starting to ask this Indian lady here if she might like to join the team.'

He turned round to face her. 'It's all right now, we've . . .'

He stopped in mid-sentence. The Asian woman had completely disappeared.

20

I pick up my pen between fingers that have now turned almost numb with cold. 'So, what you're saying is that we ought to decide how many points to give not by how much harm people do, but how important they are? I think that's stupid.'

'You see,' Marie points her pen down the list and selects the name of Queen Elizabeth I, 'when somebody asked the queen to make it illegal to become a Catholic, then she could have just said no.'

I shake my head. 'So you're suggesting that Elizabeth I was more to blame than the man who actually killed her.'

'Of course she was. You see,' Marie insists, 'we need to take account of what jobs people do. A queen or a judge would be more important than beggars – they've got more responsibility. That's why they're paid so much. And if this train doesn't set off again soon, I'm going to freeze to death and the train driver will be responsible because he's the one who's been going so slowly and now he's just walked off and left us on our own.'

I peer out of the window but there's no sign of the driver. 'It might not be his fault. It might be the person whose job it is to clear snow off the line.'

'They don't have people to clear snow off the lines.'

'Well then, I think it's time they did.'

I gaze at the soft, fluffy snow curving over the edge of the platform. 'Just think – if we were sitting at home, we'd think it was really nice.'

'I know. We'd be sitting in front of the fire with our

mugs of hot soup and our roasted chestnuts and things, wanting to go out and make snowmen.'

'Who's that?'

At the front of the train, by the driver's cab, a second figure clambers down. We watch him pull his hat down over his ears and stand his collar up around his neck. We can see his silhouette quite clearly in the station lights – his long, beaky nose and his round, fat stomach . . .

'The penguin!' chortles Marie. She peers outside as he pads across the platform. 'The penguin who stuck his big, fat flippers into our very last piece of fudge.' She's been mourning the loss of our last piece of fudge for the last hour and a half.

'Where's he going?'

The penguin plods through the heavy snow and strides solemnly through the station. 'He'll be going back to his home in the Arctic Circle. He's decided it'll be a lot warmer there.'

I can just see his head in the station lights as he waddles along the main road. 'Perhaps he's nipping home for a hot-water bottle.'

'Perhaps he's just dialled a pizza.'

'Or a curry.'

'Perhaps there's a fish 'n' chip shop.'

We both crane our necks. 'Well, I think there's a building over there where those lights are.'

'Hope you're right.' Marie's face brightens. 'It might be a pizza parlour.'

'There might be a telephone.' Actually, the thing I'd like most of all just now would be to phone my mum and let her know we're safe. 'We could nip out, perhaps, and phone home.'

'Let's have a proper look.' Marie puts down her pen and rises out of her seat.

I stand up as well but I'm not too keen on opening the door. 'Are you sure this is a good idea? I mean, we could freeze to death.'

But nothing can keep Marie from the prospect of a bag of fish 'n' chips. 'It can't get any colder, can it? Come on.'

I have a nasty suspicion that it can still get much, much colder but I follow Marie to the door. We slide the window down and straightaway the blizzard blows inside, biting our faces, stinging our eyes . . .

'Brrr! Hurry up and close it!'

Snowflakes bustle and scurry in all directions. The air is so cold it feels as if it's burning. In front of us we can see the station. In the frozen wasteland we can see the road and a couple of buildings with lights.

But the blustery wind and the soaking snow almost take my breath away. 'Come on, let's get it closed.'

However, there can be no mistake about it; in the second before the window closes, wafting towards us from the distant lights, floats the most appetising smell in the world. Marie and I cling to each other in ecstasy because this smell tells us that our train has stopped within a few hundred metres of a fully-functioning, freshly-frying, frizzling, sizzling fish 'n' chip shop.

*

'So, at the end of the first round, the Jolly Rogers take the lead with five points . . .'

A resounding cheer broke out in the Railway Tavern. 'Whooo . . . ! Whooo . . . !' Pint tankards banged on the tables; feet stamped on the wooden boards. 'Well done, lads!'

'. . . and the Flying Scotsmen are in second place with, unfortunately . . . no points at all.'

Howls of derision echoed from some of the less-than-sensitive Jolly Rogers supporters. 'Ahh! What a shame,' others cried with artificial sympathy. More than one hand was seen to pat the crates of beer and champagne bottles lying underneath the tables.

The Flying Scotsmen, marooned inside their corner, muttered miserably. 'We'll have to try an' pull us socks up,' Les encouraged his team. 'Come on, lads. Get your thinkin' caps on.'

'We'd 'ave been better off wi' that Asian woman,' complained Ken.

'What Asian woman?' asked Carter.

'And now for the second round . . .' Granville's voice crackled through the microphone, 'a question on capacity . . .'

'What's he say?' asked Ken.

'I think he said capital cities,' said Les. 'We should be all right on that.'

'What Asian woman?' Carter repeated.

'Over by the bar. I was just askin' her to come an' join us when Les walked in.' Ken pursed his lips together and nodded regretfully. 'I'd just offered to buy her . . .'

'Can anyone tell me what liquid measure is the equivalent to 0.568 of a litre.'

'That's a funny capital,' said Ken. 'I've never 'eard of it.'

Carter frowned. 'Asian women don't normally drink in pubs.'

'They don't normally come in pubs at all,' added Les. 'At least – not on their own.'

'What was she drinking?'

'Can you repeat the question please?'

'Yes,' offered Carter, 'what was she drinking?'

'Can anyone tell me what liquid measure is the

111

equivalent to 0.568 of a litre?' Granville helpfully repeated.

'Well?' asked Carter during the ensuing silence.

'Oh,' said Ken. 'A pint.'

'Very good,' crackled Granville. 'First question right! A measure of 0.568 of a litre is the equivalent of one British pint. And that gives the first point to the Flying Scotsmen.'

A clatter of grudging applause. Voices quietened as the Jolly Rogers began to lose a tiny glimmer of their confidence.

'And now,' said Granville, 'I wonder if any of the Flying Scotsmen can tell me the meaning of the word "gargantuan"?'

Silence. Tension mounted as everyone waited. 'Is it a kind of cheese?' Ken suggested.

'No, no. That's gorgonzola,' said Carter.

'How about somebody from Gargantua,' suggested Les.

Ken screwed up his eyes with the effort of thinking so hard.

'What did she look like?' asked Carter as he waited for inspiration.

'She was very big,' answered Ken.

'Sorry?'

Ken opened his arms wide above his head to demonstrate the considerable height and size of the Asian woman. 'Very big.'

'And – taken from the fictional giant king Gargantua *very big* is the right answer. And that makes a total of two points for the Flying Scotsmen.'

★

'I think there's somebody getting on the train.'

As the station is so deserted, there seems something strangely sinister about the dark figure heading across the snow towards our carriage.

'Who is it?'

I can only see the large shadow of someone's head and shoulders looming past the window. 'I don't know. I can't see properly.'

'Perhaps it's the buffet.'

'I don't think they're carrying anything.'

Marie and I both turn and stare towards the door.

What we've decided to do is make our way along the train to find out who's in charge. Then we're going to ask them if they mind just waiting while we nip out and use the telephone. We're going to say: Is this train going to be standing here for very long? Because – if you don't mind – we'd like to just nip out and telephone our parents because they might be getting worried.

Of course, I'm well aware that my mum will be getting very worried indeed. We did both phone home when we were in the café, just after we'd eaten our pancakes, but that was several hours ago.

So we're going to find a payphone, then rush inside the chip shop and order two portions of fish 'n' chips 'n' mushy peas with curry sauce and rissoles. Or battered sausage. We're taking my bag to put the chips in so they don't get cold.

'We were expectin' him 'alf an 'our ago,' says a strange voice with a Yorkshire accent.

Marie and I turn and stare at each other. We reel from the icy draught as the carriage door suddenly opens and the dark figure clambers on to the train.

'If you think you'd like to join the team, we'd be more than pleased to have you.'

We stare in amazement at the woman's soaking wet sari and Doc Martens boots. Instead of the high-pitched squeak, she now speaks with a deep man's voice. It is the same woman, though. Who else would stand gazing at the luggage rack for several seconds, then announce: 'I don't know if you might be any good at Geography . . .'

When the luggage rack makes no reply, she adds, 'I could get you a pint in if you like . . .'

Marie and I stand with our mouths wide open as the Asian woman strides along the carriage.

'How on earth did she get here?'

Marie just stands and shakes her head as the woman exits through the far door. 'You don't think she's . . . *following* us?'

'She can't be. How would she know where we are?'

I just can't understand it. 'And how did she get here?' I gaze towards the station. 'There weren't even any footprints on the platform when we arrived. I mean, she can't have got here by train.'

'Well, I wouldn't have thought there'd be any buses.'

'She must be absolutely soaked.'

'And frozen!'

We wait for a second in case the strange woman comes back, but the doors stay firmly closed.

'Are we still walking down, then?' asks Marie.

I nod reluctantly; I feel less enthusiastic about walking down the train again now. 'What are we going to say?'

'I can't remember. *Is this train going to be waiting here very long because we'd like to nip out and find a phone.*'

'I wonder where that woman's sitting, though.' I gaze apprehensively through the window into the next compartment.

'Well, at least it's not with us,' said Marie, trying hard

to joke about it. 'She might have made us both join in the team. She gives an exaggerated impersonation of the woman's new Yorkshire acccent. 'Dus tha know aught about Geography? 'Cos tha can be in our team if tha dus.'

There's a sense or relief about having something to giggle about again as we file past the rows of empty seats. 'It's bad enough sitting here, starving, in the freezing cold . . .'

'. . . without having to join in a team of lunatics.'

21

'So, at the end of the third round, the Jolly Rogers lead with fifteen points . . .'

Cheers, stamps, applause and cries of 'Whooo, whooo, whooo!' from the crowd in the Railway Tavern.

'. . . and in second place, with a score of ten points, our visiting team, the Flying Scotsmen.'

A grudging smatter of applause from some of the more polite customers, accompanied by cries of 'What a shame!' and 'Oh dear' and lots of 'Aaaghs'.

Ken and Carter did their best to ignore the groans of false sympathy as they waited for Les to bring their drinks back from the bar.

'So,' Carter recapped, 'there was this huge Asian woman standing on her own at the bar, drinking a pint of beer. Have I got that right?'

Ken nodded.

Carter was still puzzled. He'd never known an Asian woman drink pints of beer in a pub on her own before. 'What was she wearing?'

'Here we are, two pints of bitter, one mug of coffee for me.' Les placed the drinks down on the table. 'Are we all set?'

Ken and Carter tried to look enthusiastic.

'Let's see 'f we can catch up. We want to leave 'ere with that there trophy.'

Carter was still awaiting Ken's reply. 'She was wearing one of those long Indian things.' He mimed an imaginary cavernous hood going over his head, before sweeping his hands down towards the floor.

'You mean a sari?'

'That's right. Sort of red colour with black swirly bits.'

Carter's hand paused for a second as he picked up his beer.

'And now the penultimate round of the quiz. First of all, with five points to catch up, we start off with a question for the Flying Scotsmen . . .'

'What did she have on her feet?' asked Carter.

'A question on occupations. Can anyone tell me the British name for the American stevedore . . . ?'

Les bit his lip then took a long drink of his coffee. 'Steve who did he say?'

'Steve Dore. Never heard of 'im.'

Carter pointed down at his boots. 'What did she have on her feet?' he repeated.

'Oh.' Ken thought for a second. 'Dockers.'

'Quite correct. And a docker is another name for the American stevedore. One point.'

Muted applause from the regulars.

Carter was becoming a bit more agitated. 'Didn't you get a proper look at her face?' he asked.

'No, no. Her face was covered up.'

'Can anyone tell me the name of a unit of measurement used in printing, equal to one sixth of an inch?'

'I don't know nothing about printing,' admitted Ken.

Les shook his head. 'I do joined-up writin' myself.'

The atmosphere tightened as everyone leant forward, waiting for the team's reply.

Ken and Les and Carter stared at each other blankly. Both of them raised their eyebrows and looked hopefully at Carter.

Carter once again tried to look intelligent. He screwed his eyes up tightly as if in deep thought. 'Em . . .'

'Very good indeed,' declared Granville. Em is the correct answer and another point for the Flying Scotsmen.'

And a round of applause from the regulars.

*

We reach the doors to the next carriage. 'I think she'll be one of those *Care in the Community* people,' I explain. 'We've got a lot of those round our way.'

As we walk into the area in between the carriages we catch a glimpse of a figure walking down towards us. Marie grabs my arm and pulls me back. The doors bite together before they've even opened.

'What . . . ?'

There are big windows in the doors, and through them I can see a figure walking towards us. She's wearing a long black habit with a band of white round her face. She has a long hooked nose and a look of grim determination. I gulp. 'It *is* her.'

'Are you sure?'

Of course, I can't be absolutely certain, but just to be on the safe side I drag Marie towards the toilet on our left. I push the door partway open, then stop. The door's blocked by the Asian woman. I can see the red silk of her soaking sari. 'Oops, sorry . . .' I quickly close the door.

But Marie's already tugging on my sleeve, dragging us both into the other toilet opposite. This one, thank goodness, is empty. We stagger inside, squash ourselves together, lock the door then stand with our hands pressed tightly across our mouths, motionless.

Marie's fingers part. 'Was it her?' she hisses.

'I don't know,' I whisper. 'It looked like her.'

'Did she see us?'

I shake my head. 'I don't think so.'

At that moment, there's the shuffling of the doors behind us. Marie and I huddle closely together, our hands across our lips. We stand like two frozen models in the automata museum until we hear the doors open and close again.

Both of us breathe out a long, long sigh of relief. 'I don't see how it can be her,' Marie insists. 'It must have been a different nun.'

I purse my lips.

'You didn't get a proper look, did you?' Marie places her hand on the door handle. 'I'll peep out and have a look.'

'No. Don't.' I drag her back.

'She won't see me.'

'She sees everything.' We wait and listen. After a few seconds, there's the sound of the other toilet door being opened. I hold tightly to Marie as we hear the compartment doors swishing open and closed again.

'If it is Sister Frances, we won't be able to fetch our chips.'

We listen again but the only sound is the wind, gusting the snow outside. 'I know what,' suggests Marie, 'we could get off the train just here then walk down the platform to where the driver sits, then get on again.'

I shake my head. 'She might be looking out of the window. And anyway, what if the train sets off?'

Just at that moment the train gives a little jolt, as if somebody's taken off the brake. Then it makes a scraping, juddering noise, the kind of grating sound Sister Frances makes when she's trying to turn the school minibus round.

'Oh, that must be the driver,' Marie moans. 'So much for our fish 'n' chips!'

There's another jolt, a bigger one that sends us toppling forward. We have to hold on to each other to steady ourselves. Then there's a crackle from the tannoy and what sounds like a little chuckle.

'What was that?'

Marie opens the toilet door a tiny fraction and peers out into the corridor.

'Can you see anything?'

She shakes her head.

We both listen.

'Do you think we ought to go back and sit down?'

Another crackle.

'I bet the driver's been out for some chips,' suggests Marie. 'That crackle's him taking the paper off.'

'I bet that's why he stopped the train just here,' I add. 'Just to get some chips.'

The sound is followed by another little chuckle. Marie's still peeping out of the door. I reach out and hold her arm. I don't want her to leave. Of course, there's nothing scary about the sound of someone laughing. But I feel the blood slowly draining out of my neck and out of my face.

Heheeheee.

It's the kind of chuckle a six-year-old would make as he unpacks the brand-new train set he's just been given for Christmas.

Heheeheee.

But why should it be coming out of the loudspeaker on a train that's stopped in the middle of nowhere?'

Another jolt.

'Come on,' says Marie, 'we'd better go back.'

We creep out of the toilet. I peep through the window in the door, but the station is still deserted. The nearest we get to human company is the row of footprints in the snow, the contours gently blurring as their hollows fill with freshly falling flakes.

The train judders again as the engine rumbles into life. 'Well, it looks like we're ready for off.'

'Perhaps they've sent us a new driver,' I suggest.

'Perhaps he's just been to collect the buffet trolley.'

'Can you just imagine the announcement?' Marie enthuses. 'The buffet car will now be open for a selection of light refreshments . . .'

But the sound that crackles out of the loudspeaker isn't an anouncement about the buffet car. In fact, it's not an announcement at all. It's the sound of a man's voice – singing:

Down by the station, early in the morning . . .

I can feel the hairs standing upright on the back of my neck and right along my arms.

See the little puffer-trains, all in a row . . .

I gaze outside as we slowly pull away from the rosy glow of the station lights and the snow-encrusted platform.

See the little driver blow his little whistle . . .

Marie and I stand speechless as the train begins to rumble along into the empty darkness:

Whooo . . . whoooo . . . whooo . . . Off we go!

22

'And, coming up in a couple of minutes, the final round of the competition with both teams running neck and neck.'

The tension in the Railway Tavern was tangible. The Jolly Rogers had won the quiz for the last three years and had no intention whatsoever of being beaten by a bunch of buffoons from south of Barnsley. Dirty looks were being cast in the direction of the Flying Scotsmen; a stray foot had almost tripped Carter as he walked back from the bar with the drinks. 'We're doin' all right, lads,' Les tried to encourage the team. 'If we carry on like this . . .'

Ken removed the screwed-up crisp packet which had just landed on his head. He glowered round the room but couldn't see the culprit. 'If we carry on like this, we'll want to get home pretty sharpish afterwards,' he observed. 'They don't seem very keen on us in 'ere.'

'Can't think why,' said Les.

'And we'll be starting off with another round of questions for the Flying Scotsmen . . .'

'Right, thinking caps on.'

'You know,' said Carter confidentially, as he took another swig of his beer, 'I've been thinkin' about this woman.'

'What for?' asked Ken. 'We've got more important things to worry about.'

Carter frowned and shook his head. 'What I've been wondering . . .'

'And we begin with a question on Sport . . .'

'Oh no!'

'Not Sport!'

'What I've been thinking is . . .' Carter tried again.

'Shhh.'

'At which British stadium were the World Student Games held in 1992?'

'We ought to know this one,' ventured Ken. 'Wan't it somewhere in Sheffield?'

'I think you're right.'

Les clenched his fists together to help his concentration, but when he saw the Jolly Rogers supporters glaring belligerently at him he smiled politely, letting his fist drop into a little half-hearted wave.

Carter had been sitting in silent contemplation, his head deep in his hands. Suddenly he looked up, his face bright and animated. 'I might be wrong, but . . .'

'Yes?'

'That woman . . .'

'Oh no. Not her again. Come on, Carter, we've got other things to think about.'

'But . . .'

'Come on,' said Les. 'Get your thinkin' cap on. Name of a stadium. Erm . . .'

'Sorry, team, I'll have to hurry you up.'

'What I'm thinking, though,' said Carter, 'is that it might actually be Don Valley.'

'And the British stadium where the World Student Games were held in 1992 was . . . Don Valley in Sheffield. Very good indeed.'

One sad, solitary supporter in a far corner of the room began an outburst of enthusiastic applause. He was quickly stifled by a barrage of dirty looks from the Jolly Rogers supporters.

'Well done, lads. Very good,' said Les.

'Haven't I heard that name before?' asked Ken.

Just then, the Railway Tavern door opened and a snow-covered figure waddled wetly into the bar. His bulging stomach formed a shelf on which snow had settled thickly, giving him an even more penguin-like appearance.

'Looks like the Abominable Snowman.'

'What's that red light in the middle of his face?'

'I think it's supposed to be his nose.'

'And the second question is: what is the name of the Irish missionary in Northumbria who founded the monastery at Lindisfarne?'

The question met with a stunned silence from the team.

But Carter was becoming more and more animated. 'The bloke the police are looking for,' he explained.

'He didn't go an' start a monastery, did he?' asked Les.

'Well, it's one way of givin' 'em the slip,' suggested Ken.

'No, no. The chap who escaped from our place.'

Orgreave trudged towards the telephone posted beside the bar. When there was no one standing in front of it, he stared round vacantly. When he couldn't see anything at all he took his glasses off and wiped them with a greasy corner of his chip wrapper.

'Oh,' said Les. 'You mean St Aiden's.'

'And the name of the Irish missionary who founded the monastery at Lindisfarne is . . . St Aiden. Very well answered. And that brings the Flying Scotsmen into the lead!'

There was no applause whatsoever as everyone poised

on the edges of their seats, anxious to see what would happen next.

What happened next was that Orgreave at last caught sight of Les and Ken and dripped his way towards them between the crates of beer and the champagne bottles. His squelching footsteps were the only interruption to the silence shrouded across the room.

'Oh good gracious me. It's Orgreave,' said Les. 'How do. Didn't recognise you under all that snow.'

Orgeave tried to open his mouth but his jaw appeared to be temporarily frozen.

'I just bumped into one or two of my mates. Just havin' a cup o' coffee. Do you fancy a sit down?'

Orgreave was so numb with cold that he found it difficult to speak. He clung on to the chips wrapped snugly inside his jacket as a child might have cuddled a teddy.

'You all right?'

As the temperature rose round Orgreave's bag of chips, the snow on his jacket began to melt and slither into a small avalanche. It picked up speed as it slid down his jacket and splodged into Ken's glass of beer.

'Watch what you're doin',' said Les. 'They water the beer down enough in 'ere already.'

Orgreave tried again to open his mouth.

'You feelin' all right?'

Frozen words eventually began spluttering like hailstones out of Orgreave's mouth. 'I'm all right,' he explained to Les. 'I'm fine. It's just the . . . well, I'm just a bit worried about the train . . . '

'Train? Why? What's up with it? It's still there in't it?'

Orgreave felt a bit stupid as he stood there shaking his head. When no one seemed to take him seriously, he felt as though he somehow had to explain. 'I wondered if you might have been out an' moved it.'

'Moved it? How do you mean?'

Another splodge of melted snow dripped from Orgreave's nose into Les's mug of coffee. 'Well,' he said, feeling even more stupid than ever, 'because well . . . because it just doesn't seem to be there any more.'

*

The train picks up speed. It rumbles along as Marie and I are buffeted and rocked from side to side. I glance outside at the snow-banked hills and hedges as ghostly flakes flit past the window.

'Well, this makes a change,' Marie declares, as the train rolls along even faster. 'Perhaps we'll get home tonight after all.'

I peer outside again, but the landscape is now blurred into a pale and eerie light. There are no definite shapes – no familiar buildings, nothing for us to recognise at all.

'We could be anywhere, couldn't we?' says Marie.

And, of course, that's true.

We stagger with difficulty down the aisle as we're heaved and rocked about. 'Whoops!' I grab one of the headrests to regain my balance as I nearly topple over.

'Well, I just hope the driver can see where he's going,' says Marie. 'I wouldn't have thought visibility would be all that good.'

But the train rolls forward oblivious of the blizzard and the huge, thick banks of snow.

I can see our table in front of us with our papers and fudge box and pens spread out. We lean for a moment against one of the padded headrests as we swerve round a bend.

There's another surreptitious chuckle from the speaker.

'They ought to make some proper announcements,' I complain.

'I know.'

We arrive at our table and collapse into our places by the window. I glance back towards the door to make sure we've not been followed. 'At least that strange woman's disappeared.'

'She'll be sitting with Sister Frances.'

'Praying for our safe arrival.' Both of us chuckle but, as the white, blurred landscape rushes past, with no clue at all of where we are or where we're going, the idea of praying for our safe arrival doesn't seem such a bad idea.

'I wonder why she didn't sit in here?' says Marie. 'There's plenty of spare seats.'

It's when Marie talks about the woman sitting down that I suddenly start to wonder.

'I wonder why she was . . .' I stop in mid-sentence.

'What?'

I hold on to the edge of the table as the train gives another lurch. 'I'm just wondering why she was . . . standing up.'

'What do you mean . . . standing up?'

'In the toilet.'

Marie just blinks incomprehendingly.

'She was standing up, wasn't she?'

Marie nods.

'In the loo.'

'So?'

Of course, Marie's never had a little brother who needs taking to the toilet every few hours, so it doesn't immediately occur to her that it's only boys and men who stand with their backs to the door and . . . 'If she was a woman, she'd have been sitting down.'

Marie frowns. 'She might have been combing her hair, though, or putting her lipstick on.'

I sigh. 'Would that be the first thing she'd do when she came in out of the blizzard?'

Marie thinks for a moment. 'I don't know.'

Suddenly, everything falls into place. 'Just look how big she is and how deep her voice is and . . . we've never seen her face, have we? That's why she keeps it covered up.'

'You mean, she might have a long grey beard and whiskers?'

I grin. 'She might have. I bet she was just pretending to do that squeaky voice.'

'Well then, why is she wearing woman's clothes?'

'I don't know.'

I gaze down the empty carriage, back towards the door. I don't want to admit it to Marie, but I'm starting to feel quite shaky. I don't actually feel scared of the strange Asian woman, but I do feel uneasy about a man who might be a lunatic who dresses as a woman and always keeps his face concealed. I just stare out of the window and say nothing.

Marie presses her nose against the glass. 'It's just like Narnia,' she enthuses. 'Just think – we could have walked through the back of a wardrobe and here we are in a snow-locked landscape covered in frost and icicles, with everything just like a fairy grotto.'

Marie makes it sound like a winter wonderland but there now seems something much more sinister about a landscape where nothing is familiar, where there's no sign of any living soul. Where, in fact, the only people we've seen at all in the last hour are the two figures departing swiftly from our train, an unnamed nun and the strange man dressed as a woman who doesn't want us to see his face.

There's another crackling on the tannoy. I feel a shiver down my spine as the now-familiar voice starts to sing:

The runaway train came down the track and she blew,
whooo . . .

Because it suddenly occurs to me that we might have made a terrible mistake. We were afraid of getting off the train and going to the chip shop because we were scared of being left behind, scared that the train might go without us.

The runaway train came down the track and she blew,
whooo . . .

We assumed that the danger was out there in the blizzard and in the snow-locked landscape but what if . . . ?

The runaway train came down the track,
Her whistle wide and her throttle back . . .

But what if the snow-locked landscape was the safest place to be? What if the only really dangerous place is right here on this train?

I suddenly reach forward and grab Marie by the hand because, just at that minute, all the lights go out.

And she blew, blew, blew, blew blew.

23

'Can anyone tell me the name of the string of islands located off the southern tip of Florida?'

Ken and Les and Carter didn't stare blankly at each other. They stared blankly at Orgreave, snow-drenched and dripping in front of their table. 'What do you mean?' asked Les. 'The train doesn't seem to be there any more?'

Orgreave, numb with cold, stood so stiffly he looked more like a penguin than ever. 'Haven't you been an' moved it?'

Ken and Les and Carter gazed at each other.

'Where's the keys?' Ken asked Les.

Les began searching through his pockets. 'They're 'ere somewhere. I had 'em when I come in.'

'You had 'em at the bar,' Ken recollected. 'That was the first thing you did when you walked in – you put 'em down on the bar.'

Les stood up and waved to get the attention of the barman. Then he pointed to the bar and mimed opening a lock with a large key.

The barman frowned and shook his head.

'You must 'ave looked in the wrong place,' Ken explained to Orgreave.

Orgreave was tempted to explain that the only place to look for the train was standing on the railway line somewhere in front of the station but he thought it best to say nothing.

'The name of the string of islands located off the southern tip of Florida . . . ?'

Les waved at the barman again but he'd already begun to serve another customer.

Les checked his pockets once more then shouted across to the bar, 'Keys!'

'Very good. Florida Keys is the right answer. Now, question two.'

But it was Carter who was becoming most upset. He stood up and began to thread his way towards the bar. 'Excuse me.'

'And the next question for the Flying Scotsmen . . .'

'Where's he goin'?' asked Ken.

'I don't know,' said Les. 'Come on, Carter,' he shouted. 'Let's get this last question finished first.'

But Carter was talking to the barman. 'Have you picked up a set of keys? They were left out on the bar.'

The barman shook his head.

'Did you see an Asian woman – in a sari?'

'. . . What is the name of the thirty-ninth president of the United States of America?'

The barman nodded. 'I could hardly miss her – asked for a pint of bitter.'

'Did she say anything else?'

'She went on about my reporting incidents to the police. I don't know where she'd got that from. I'm not a police informer.'

'Then what?'

'Come on, lads,' urged Les. 'Last question. Dun't anybody know?'

The barman thought for a moment. 'She picked up a set of keys,' he recollected. 'They were lying on the bar. She picked them up just before she walked out of the door.'

'Oh no!'

Ken didn't know the answer. Les didn't know and

Orgreave was frozen into silence. They all turned to Carter standing by the bar. 'Carter!' they shouted in unison.

'And the thirty-ninth president of the United States was . . . Jimmy Carter! Very well answered, the Flying Scotsmen. And that completes the . . .'

Carter picked up the phone by the bar and started to dial the number of St Aiden's.

*

'Do you think there might have been a power cut?'

If there was a power cut, I don't think the train would still be running but I don't know how else to explain the complete and total blackness. 'I don't know.'

Marie and I cling tightly to each other's arms as the train plunges forward.

'Do you think he might be drunk?' suggests Marie.

'I don't know.'

'He might have been out for a drink while we were waiting in the station – he might have nipped off to the pub.'

'You're not supposed to drink and drive.'

'I know.'

I thought it would be hard for us to survive the journey in the awful cold. I thought it would be hard for us to survive without anything to eat apart from a box of Dungeon fudge. I thought it would be hard for us to survive a train journey with a strange woman who we think is a man who may or may not be following us. But now we've survived all that only to be hurtled along in total darkness, by a man who appears to be completely drunk.

The runaway train came down the track and she blew, whoooo . . .

132

Of course, now that the lights of the station have been left such a long, long way behind, everything around us is completely black. If someone walked down the train and stood right in front of us, we wouldn't be able to see them. The only light is from the pale and ghostly pallor reflected outside the glass.

The runaway train came down the track and she blew,
whooo . . .

Apart from the fact that, away in front of us, I can see a tiny pinprick of red. It looks like the weeny light I have on the sound system in my room to tell me when I've left it switched on at night. 'I think that's a red signal.'

'Where?'

I point.

'I can't see anything.'

'We'll be slowing down again now.'

But the train just rolls along faster.

Marie peers through the window. 'I still can't see anything. Are you sure . . . ?'

I look again. What else is red and lights up and stands next to the railway line?

'. . . because we seem to be going faster than ever.'

I tighten my grip on her arm as our carriage swerves round the bend.

'Perhaps it's the signal for a different line.'

I don't like to say so, but I rather suspect that there is no different line. We haven't passed any other trains. Not that I've noticed, anyway.

'I wonder if . . .'

'What?'

'What if the driver's got so drunk that he hasn't seen the signal?'

There's a dryness in my throat. I try not to think about the awful possibility. 'No. Of course he won't

133

have.' But really, my heart is sinking. I don't know what to think.

'Anyway, if we carry on like this, we'll be home in ten or fifteen minutes.' I know Marie's just trying to keep cheerful.

I cling again to the edge of the table as we're thrown from side to side. Maybe we are hurtling along much faster than we've travelled all day, but this is the furthest I've felt so far from our nice, cosy living room at home and my mum, lifting the corner of the curtains, watching for me walking up the path.

I peer outside to look for the signal, but the view is a streak of white – buildings and hedges blending together in a sickening blur.

Suddenly there's a squeal of brakes. My head is thrown right back, jerking my neck. I cling hold of the armrest and brace myself as the brakes make a terrible screech. The sound is like a scream. The train grinds to a halt with Marie and myself thrown forward, our ribs jammed hard against the table, our pens and papers sliding to the floor. The carrier bags clatter to our feet, the fudge box skims into space and my stomach lurches with panic.

I close my eyes for several seconds as circles of red spin round and round inside my head. My heart beats like a drum machine. I hold Marie's hand as I take a deep breath. 'Are you OK?'

'Mmmm.' Marie's hand is cold and fluttering like a frightened bird. 'Are you all right?'

I think so. 'Yes, Yes, I'm OK.'

'Perhaps that was the signal.'

I swallow. 'But we saw it ages ago.'

'I know.'

I try to think of something we can do. But all we can do is sit and wait as the engine grates and rumbles.

'Shall we find all our stuff?'

I nod, but neither of us wants to move. We both sit, clinging tightly to each other's arms.

'Do you think we've broken down?'

'I don't know.'

Marie gives a long, drawn-out sigh. 'We'll never find our things now, will we? Not in the dark. We'll have to wait for the lights to come back on.'

I gaze at the blackness around us. We could be waiting for a long, long time. 'What if the lights have broken?'

Marie sighs again. Then she reaches down and starts to grope around her feet. 'I can't feel anything.'

'Come on. Let's look properly.'

We slide out of our seats and fumble round the aisle. 'I've found my rucksack,' Marie announces.

'Here's Sister's candle.'

'There's another judder from the engine. We pause, both holding tightly to the table.

'I know,' suggests Marie. 'We can light the candle.'

'No we can't. It's a sacred candle, for lighting in a church. We can't just light it to see where we are.'

There's a pause. 'It *is* an emergency,' says Marie.

I don't say anything.

'We can use it to find all our things. See if you can feel the matches.'

I begin to spread my hands around the floor as the engine splutters into life. 'Hope they haven't got wet.'

I locate the matches underneath my seat. 'Do you think Sister'll mind?'

'It doesn't matter,' says Marie, opening the box. 'We can always buy another candle when we get home.' She strikes the match and lights the candle at the first attempt.

'That's better.' The yellow glow of the candlelight transforms the nightmare blackness into a cosy scene that spells homeliness and safety.

'Find the fudge box. We can use that to stand it on.'

With the lighted candle, we can easily find the rest of our belongings. I drip candle wax on the fudge box lid then stand the candle upright. 'There we are!'

'We could have a party.'

'Oh yes. All we need's a bit more food and drink . . .'

'And some more people . . .'

'Some music . . .'

'A sound system . . .'

'And a fire.'

We both sit back in our places again as the train begins to move. 'Well, here we go,' says Marie.

As I look outside, I realise that the train is definitely moving – the only problem is that now we're going backwards.

24

'It happened on Bonfire Night,' Ken explained, 'when Donald was just a little lad.'

They were skidding away in the Smile-Away minibus – Ken and Carter seated in the front, Les and Orgreave in the back, resting their feet on the crates of beer which the landlord had helped them to slide away from the scuttled crews of Jolly Rogers.

'What started everything off, you see, was that Rivelin, Donald's mother, had run away with a travelling salesman from Wath-on-Dearne.'

'I wouldn't trust anybody from Wath-on-Dearne,' remarked Les. 'They weren't too friendly I remember when we won the semifinal.'

'Anyway, Loxley didn't want to give up his job as an engine driver, but it wasn't easy for him to look after little Donald all by himself.'

Everyone nodded as Carter swerved around a corner into a narrow, winding lane.

'Of course,' Ken went on, 'Loxley was absolutely devastated when his wife left, but he was a good bloke. He was determined to 'ang on to the little lad. People said he ought to 'ave 'im adopted or taken into care – there weren't so many single dads about in them days, people thought it was more of a woman's job, bringin' up a little kid – but Loxley insisted he could manage. He had a brother – an 'ospital porter – and Loxley's brother an' his wife used to look after Don in the school holidays.'

Carter scraped the gears as he tried to coax the minibus

up the icy stretch of road. 'So, how do you know about all this?'

'Like I said, I used to work with him,' Ken explained. 'I didn't know 'im well, like, but we were in the same depot.'

'Try changin' into second,' Les advised. 'Just keep moving, though. Don't let it stop.'

Carter grated the gears yet again as the engine reluctantly spluttered up the hill. 'Go on,' he encouraged Ken.

'Well, there were some occasions – not many, mind you – when Loxley just couldn't find anybody to look after Donald. What he used to do was take the little lad in with 'im to work.'

Carter shook his head. 'But weren't there some . . . like, safety regulations?'

Ken nodded. 'We all kept quiet about it, you see. We didn't want to get him into trouble and the little lad – well, he just loved trains. He was in his element. He used to go an' visit the signalmen in the signal box – they'd always give him some sweets – an' the chap who worked the level crossing. But there was nothing he liked better than actually sitting up there in the cab, pretending he was drivin' a train.'

'You mean Loxley actually allowed Don to sit in the cab when he was driving?'

Ken nodded. 'We knew it was a bit dangerous but we didn't think there was much harm. He had a special little harness, like a safety belt, which Loxley had made for 'im. Anyway,' Ken gazed out at the deserted landscape, 'as I was saying, it was Bonfire Night . . .'

*

'Well, what I think we ought to do now we've got the

138

candles,' suggests Marie, 'is walk down and find the nun and see whether it really is Sister Frances.'

The candlelight casts a spooky glow around the carriage. We've stacked our shopping bags on the floor in case of any more unscheduled stops; but we've kept out the box of matches and the other candle that I bought from the Dungeon. It stands on the table between us, shaped like a cute tiny skeleton, waving cheerfully as he clambers out of his coffin. 'We won't be scared walking through the carriages now, will we? Not when we've lit both the candles.'

I say nothing. I don't think it's true that we won't be scared, but at least walking down the train will be doing something positive. What I don't want to do any longer is just sit here, listening to the crackling, infantile songs, as we lurch and brake and bump and screech, wondering if, or when, we might crash. What I want is to meet some sensible adults who can explain to us just what's going on.

The runaway train came down the track and she blew,
whooo . . .

'Do you think we'll bump into that loony man/woman or whatever it is?'

Marie frowns. 'I don't know, but we might find the nun first.' She picks up the candle. 'Do you really think it was Sister?'

The runaway train came down the track and she blew,
whooo . . .

I purse my lips.

'I mean, you didn't see her properly, did you?'

'It did look like her.'

'I know but, what would she be doing up here? I mean, she'd have been at school, wouldn't she? Or in her car.'

The runaway train came down the track,
Her whistle wide and her throttle back . . .

I shrug my shoulders. I don't think there can be all that many people – let alone all that many nuns – who look just like Sister Frances. 'If it is her, I don't think it'll matter about not wearing our uniform. I mean, she might be more worried about us all getting home all right.'

Marie doesn't look too sure. 'She'll know we haven't lit the candle in the convent . . .'

And she blew, blew, blew, blew, blew.

I glance down at the candle in Marie's outstretched hand. There doesn't really seem much point in pretending to Sister that we went and bought another one. 'Well, like you say, it's an emergency.' I hold out my hand. 'Come on. Let's light the other candle.'

'OK. Don't waste matches, though. We've only got two left.' Marie holds out her candle for me to light the little skeleton. 'Cute, isn't he?'

I light the wick protruding from the top of the coffin and the small round, grinning skull begins to glow. I cup my palms one at a time above the flame so that my hands can defrost.

'Let's give him a name.'

I smile. 'What goes with skeleton? Sydney. Sydney the skeleton.'

'We can pretend we're in the Dungeon.' Marie takes hold of my hand as we begin to walk out into the aisle. 'Exciting, isn't it?'

The candlelight forms long, looming shadows as it transforms our carriage into something more like a spooky ghost train ride.

'Do you think the driver can actually see where he's going?' asks Marie, as we begin to pick up speed again. 'Trains don't normally go backwards, do they?'

I've got no idea. 'Well, we're going really fast now. He ought to be able to see.'

We stagger forward, through the shadows, Marie first with the large candle, then Sydney and myself. It would be nice to think that it's as fun and exciting as Marie likes to pretend, but as I explained earlier, the only really exciting things are when you know that it's only make-believe – like in horror films and videos when you know it's only people acting. When things are really happening, when real people are being tortured or when you're creeping along a runaway train driven backwards by a drunken driver in the dark, it isn't fun at all. You just feel very, very scared.

I have to drop Marie's hand for a while because my candle starts to flicker. I cup my palm around the flame. 'Hope it doesn't blow out.'

The doors to the next carriage open by themselves as we approach. We walk through one at a time, holding up our candles and gazing round.

'Where is everybody?'

I peer along the aisle, checking every seat, hoping to see some signs of civilization – some warm and friendly faces or at least shopping bags, abandoned crisp packets, newspapers or magazines.

The tables however, are stark and bare; the only faces we see are our reflections, quaking in the candlelight, staring back at us from the windows.

25

'November the fifth,' Ken explained, 'Donald's school was closed. I don't know why. But this was one of those days when his father didn't have anywhere to leave him. All I know is, he took the little lad on the train with him, strapped inside his harness in the cab.'

'We're gettin' a bit low on petrol, aren't we?' Les interrupted.

'Don't worry.' Carter glanced at the gauge. 'There's a spare can in the back.'

'So what happened, then?'

'Well,' said Ken, 'nobody really knows what happened on that journey. The best theory is that Loxley 'ad an 'eart attack. Nowadays, you see,' Ken suddenly realized that Carter was one of the few people he knew who was completely ignorant about the workings of a locomotive, 'all engine drivers have a pressure pad – you keep your foot on it as you drive along. If the pressure eases up – if you were to fall asleep, or have an 'eart attack or whatever, the train'd automatically slow down and stop.' He paused. 'They didn't have 'em in them days.'

'It's because of accidents like that though,' Les explained, 'that they brought 'em in.'

Ken nodded. 'So it was just one of those tragic coincidences, really. There was a train that had broken down – a passenger train full of commuters going into Birmingham. The train was just standing there – driver waitin' for instructions. Signals were at red so Loxley should have slowed down an' stopped but, as I say, no one knows what happened. The coroner said 'e'd 'ad an 'eart attack and 'e'd had that before the accident. He was thrown out o' the cab and killed outright.'

There was a long, respectful pause.

'And what about Don?' asked Carter quietly.

Ken gazed out of the window at the deserted countryside. 'Don was still strapped in. You'd 'ave expected him to be crushed to death but he wasn't. He was still sitting there in his special 'arness when the ambulances started to arrive. Of course, there was terrible carnage. Bodies everywhere – bits of bodies – terrible sight for a little lad. Terrible.' Ken shook his head. 'An' then there was 'is father . . .'

There was another long silence.

Carter tried to imagine the miniature version of Don Valley strapped into the nightmare express train. 'Wasn't Don injured?' he asked.

Ken paused. 'Well, he was cut and bruised, obviously, but they did say there was nothing else wrong. Mind you, you see, when anybody saw him afterwards, anybody from the railway – we all knew him, you see – we'd bump into 'im and say hello; signalmen, drivers, we always clubbed together to buy him a bit o' something for Christmas; we always said, between ourselves like, that he'd never been right since. We wondered if he'd had a massive bump on the 'ead an' perhaps got brain damage but nobody seemed to know. Physically, I mean, he was all there but – well, he used to be such a lively little lad . . .'

The minibus had hit a bank of snow and Carter was struggling to scrape the gears into reverse. 'What actually happened to Don, though?' he asked. 'I mean, who looked after him after his dad . . . ?'

'Take your foot off the accelerator,' offered Les. 'Just go backwards and forwards till you get it to grip.'

'Loxley's brother . . .' Ken went on, '. . . the one who was an 'ospital porter – him an' his wife, they brought him up.'

'Do you want us to get out an' shove?'

'I'll just have another go.'

'One thing,' Ken looked questioningly at Carter, 'I did wonder . . .'

'Mmm . . . ?'

'Nowadays if anything like that happens – when there's a major disaster or anything – they have therapists an' that. Counsellors. Well, of course, there was nothing like that in them days.'

Carter took his foot off the clutch as he turned to face Ken.

'Loxley's brother and his wife, they thought it best to say nothing at all about the accident. They asked us not to mention it. They told Don his father 'ad 'ad an 'eart attack – they never talked about the crash. I always felt, myself – I know they meant well but I don't think they were doin' 'im any favours.'

Carter shook his head sadly. 'Don would have been desperate to talk about it,' he explained. 'You see, if everybody refused to recognise that such a terrible thing had happened, it wouldn't make the memory go away. Don would be still desperate to live through what he remembered, struggling to come to terms with it.'

'So,' Ken concluded, 'you think that could be the reason why he's finished up gettin' 'imself obsessed with trains. You think that's why he keeps wanting to act out – like you were sayin' – all these train crashes?'

Carter nodded. 'The only problem is,' he gripped hard on the steering wheel, 'if he really is driving that train at the moment, then living out his childhood traumas is the most dangerous thing he can do . . .'

144

There was an ominous pause.

'An' what really worries me,' added Ken, 'is if there's any passengers still left on that there train with 'im . . .'

*

The train careers along at such a rate that it's like trying to walk along one of those haunted-house rides where the floor keeps moving and swaying in different directions. I roll to one side, then the other, then I grab hold of Marie and we both nearly topple down together. I'm no sooner standing upright than my candle flickers out and I have to light it again.

'Just don't let them both go out together,' Marie warns.

I peer down at little Sydney but his cheeky, cute expression has completely disappeared. The flame has melted a hollow right down through his skull as though a mad axeman's started slicing him in half. His right arm has stretched and slithered as though it's been pulled out of joint on the rack.

And, as I stagger along in the candleglow, I realise that I feel as out of joint and hollow as poor little Sydney myself. It's as if all the events of the day – the sudden snow and the Dungeon and the strange man in the Gunpowder Plot, the spooky singing on the speakers – it's as if all of them have sapped my strength. Instead of the fairly-strong person that I normally am, I feel empty and disjointed. I try not to let it show, of course, as I step forward into the gloom. We shine our candles at every row of seats we pass but all of them are empty.

We stagger through to the next carriage and this time, Marie's candle is blown out with the draught. I light it again from mine.

145

At the bottom end of the carriage, I can see some belongings left out on a table. My hopes begin to rise. 'I think there's somebody down there.'

If only we could meet someone sensible. If we came across just one nice, sympathetic adult who could explain to us what was going on, then none of this would be so scary. Sister Frances, in fact, would be a godsend.

We lurch to one side as the train veers round a bend, then, as we approach the bottom table, I make out a book and a briefcase and . . . 'There's a box of liquorice allsorts.'

'Well,' says Marie, 'I just hope there's plenty left.'

We stagger and sway towards the last table in the carriage, but there's no one sitting there. There's just a coat and a scarf left on the seat.

Marie lifts the lid of the liquorice allsort box. 'Sister Frances always takes liquorice allsorts, doesn't she, when she goes to visit Agnes?' She peeps inside. 'Oh no. Looks like she's eaten them all herself.'

We place our candles beside the large black briefcase and I gaze at the thick leather book. I can just see the border of a train ticket used as a bookmark. 'I wonder if it's a Bible.'

'Let's have a look.'

Of course, I wouldn't normally dream of looking at someone else's private possessions on a train. I gaze up and down the carriage but there's still no one about. 'Well, it is an emergency . . .'

I open the book at the place where the train ticket's been placed and I illuminate it with the candle. 'It's a ticket for Sheffield. Look. It says Adult Single.'

'And is it a Bible?'

I glance back down. '"The Lord is my Shepherd",' I read, my voice shaking slightly, '"I shall not want."

Sister's favourite psalm. "He maketh me to lie down in green pastures . . ."'

'Look in the front.'

I open the front page of the Bible and staring straight in front of me is the familiar writing that we see on all our school reports – the signature at the end of every letter we take home. 'It *is* Sister's.'

Marie turns it round to have a look. 'Perhaps she went to see Agnes and she wasn't in.'

I shake my head. 'Agnes is locked up, isn't she? She's in a high-security unit.'

'Well, perhaps Sister's car broke down.'

As I stare at Sister's familiar things – her briefcase and her Bible, her liquorice allsorts box, even her black woolly coat and scarf spread out on the seat – I feel an overwhelming sense of relief. I suddenly realise that our nightmare might be over. 'It really is her,' I say again as if I need to convince myself. 'It is her.'

'That means we're safe,' says Marie. 'Doesn't it?'

I nod, smiling, because although Sister isn't actually here in the carriage with us, we know she can't be very far away.

'Where do you think she is?'

'Well, she might have gone to look for the buffet car. Or gone to find the loo.'

Marie nods. 'We should have come to try and find her earlier. Shouldn't we?'

Of course, we should. Then we needn't have been so worried. 'I know.' I pick up dripping, slithering Sydney once again, 'Anyway, she can't be far away. We'll soon find where she's gone.'

26

'There ought to be a shovel in the back,' explained Carter, beating his fists against the steering wheel as he tried yet again to reverse the Smile-Away bus. 'The tyres just won't grip.'

'Come on then, lads,' ordered Les. 'Everybody out.'

The Flying Scotsmen, assisted by the recently-defrosted Orgreave, clambered out of the bus. The snow was now easing off, there was a bright, full moon and the fields and hedges glistened. Carter gazed around at the moonlight reflecting on the crisp, fresh snow.

'Let's get some weight behind it,' shouted Les.

In spite of the brightness of his surroundings, Carter felt as though he had a lead weight in his stomach, a feeling of deep and intense dread.

'Here we go!'

When they'd piled exultantly into the minibus with their beer, the champagne, and the John Sanella trophy, they assumed they would head off the train in no time. Les knew where a narrow country lane ran alongside the track, just next to the signal which, all the railway men insisted, would definitely be at red.

'Right, come on, lads!'

The plan was for Carter to climb inside the cab on the waiting train, talk nicely to Don and persuade him to give up the keys. After that, Les would take over the train and drive it on to Sheffield, in the hope that no one would ever find out how or why it had been left standing at an unmanned station without driver or conductor.

''ere we go!'

Les shovelled snow from round the front wheels as everyone else stood in the snowdrift, leaned on the minibus and shoved. The wheels spun in midair, flinging flurries of snow into their faces, but the Flying Scotsmen were undeterred. After a few seconds the tyres gripped and the minibus slid back to the middle of the road.

'Well done, lads!' shouted Les.

Now Carter was having very grave doubts about whether they'd ever reach the train before tragedy occurred.

'How we doin' for petrol?' asked Ken as they climbed back into their seats. Shall we put that extra can in?'

'Leave it till later,' Carter insisted. 'We mustn't waste any more time.' He slipped back into his seat, unfolded the road map and held it up towards the tiny interior light. He could just about trace the black train line with his forefinger and then the winding red squiggle that signified the road they were on. On paper, the two were less than a centimetre apart.

'We need to find a different route,' he explained to Les. 'We're just going to get blocked in by snow if we carry on down here.'

'Let's 'ave a look.'

Les screwed up his eyes as he struggled to focus on the map. 'What about this 'ere?' he pointed.

'That's a river,' explained Carter.

'We might be all right down there,' suggested Ken. 'It might be frozen over. We could slide down it.'

'What about that wiggly road down there?'

Carter scrutinised the map. 'I think that's where we spilled the vinegar off Orgreave's chips.'

'Perhaps we'd better double back to the main road then.'

Carter nodded reluctantly as he restarted the engine and passed the map to Ken. He turned to Les. 'How long do you think it'll take?'

'I don't know. No idea.'

Carter slid the minibus back towards the main road, surreptitiously wiping the sweat from underneath his armpits. Don't panic, Carter, he told himself. Keep calm. They'd set off full of enthusiasm, assuming they'd have plenty of time. But the picture Ken had conjured up of a crashed train with bodies strewn across the track caused beads of perspiration to stand out on Carter's forehead. 'Can you turn that heater down?' he asked Ken.

'Turn it down? We're only just starting to warm up.'

'It's freezing back here,' complained Orgreave. 'I think I might be suffering from frostbite.'

Carter took a deep breath and pressed his foot hard on the accelerator.

*

We're about to set off down the corridor again when there's another squeal of brakes. 'Watch out!'

The train screeches to a halt with such force that both of us are thrown right back. I grab the headrest of the seat beside me, twisting my arm.

'Help!' Marie topples to one of the seats.

My candle blows out. I manage to steady myself then, as the train skids to a stop, I collapse into the nearest seat. 'Are you all right?'

Marie grunts.

I close my eyes as my stomach lurches. I think for a moment that I'm going to be sick but then I take a deep breath. I feel shattered. I'm fairly certain that my body's still intact but I feel more like one of those cartoon

150

characters who runs headlong into a brick wall, splinters into a thousand tiny pieces and then waits for the final judder that will shatter them into a mosaic.

I take another breath.

There's now no mistaking the fact that there's something seriously wrong with this train. I don't know what we're going to do. I actually feel like bursting into tears. If I didn't have to put on a brave face in front of Marie, then I know I'd just sit down and sob.

There's a movement from the dark shape that seems to be Marie. 'Are you all right?'

'Yes. Yes, I'm fine.'

I do realise, of course, that the train has now stopped again, the engine's switched off and both our candles have blown out.

'Perhaps we should just get off.'

I feel very tempted to say yes, of course we should. In spite of the awful weather, and in spite of the fact that we've no idea where we are, I'm certain that we'd be much safer walking outside on the train tracks than being thrown about in here. 'But we've got to find Sister first, haven't we?' Of course, now we know that Sister Frances is actually on the train somewhere, we can't just get off without her.

Marie sits up. I assume she's nodding in agreement although I can't see her in the dark.

'Have you still got the matches?'

She rummages through her pockets while I hold up the remains of snivelling Sydney. The beads of wax trickle from his nose like slithers of gooey snot.

'Do you think she might have got off the train?'

'No, she wouldn't have left her coat, would she? And her Bible.'

'You don't think she might have . . .' Marie lowers

151

her voice even though there's no one about, '. . . had an accident?'

My heart turns over. Could Sister have fallen out of the train as we've rocketed round a corner? Could she have slithered out of a door as the wheels squealed to a halt? Could somebody have . . . ?

I shake my head. The thought is too horrible.

Suddenly there's a stutter, the engine bursts into life, and we begin to judder forward again.

Marie holds a match to both our candles.

'That's better.' I hold Sydney aloft to brighten up the carriage.

'Come on.' Marie takes hold of my arm and we creep along the aisle as the train lurches forward.

I walk with my candle held high, checking the slim platoons of silent, empty sets. My spirits would be raised if I could only spy a sandwich box or a sports bag, a woolly scarf or a magazine – some sign that we might not be the only people left alive.

All the tables and seats are empty.

'What's happened to everyone?'

But Marie is staring ahead at the window that looks through the next set of doors.

'What's the matter?'

'Can you see that?'

'What?'

'Just behind the door. Look.'

We both pause.

Behind the window at the end of the carriage is a large, dark shadow. We both stand still for a moment. 'Do you think it's her?'

I'm not too sure; it doesn't look like a woman somehow. But of course, it has to be. 'It must be.'

We stagger forward. I keep my eyes fixed on the dark figure, expecting it to wave or move towards us.

'Why hasn't she seen us?'

'Perhaps she's got her eyes closed.'

'Perhaps she's saying her prayers.'

It does seem a very strange place, though, for Sister to say her prayers. I mean, why doesn't she just go and sit back at her table? And if she's praying, why has she left her Bible behind?

The shadow actually seems much too large and looming to be Sister, but of course, nothing is its natural size in the candlelight.

We ease forward a bit more slowly. The circles of light from our candles constantly quiver and dance with the trembling of our hands.

I keep my eyes fixed firmly on the shape behind the door. It seems to be standing sideways on, gazing outside. Its head is definitely covered in something long and black and flowing. I open my mouth to call but my throat is too dry to speak. The sound I make is a kind of whimper.

'You all right?' Marie asks.

'Mmm.'

'It is her, isn't it?'

I nod.

I scour the remaining empty seats, still hoping that we might encounter a sensible person sitting there, eating sandwiches or listening to their Walkman or drinking coffee from a flask.

All the seats are empty.

We creep towards the doors. As they suddenly slide apart, the shadowy figure is highlighted by the candlelight. It reminds me for a second of the Bonfire Night display – the tableaux of people that were standing

153

there all the time but which lit up one at a time according to their position in the story.

The large figure has its features framed by a band of white.

'Sister . . . ?' Marie begins tentatively.

But as it turns to face us, and as its face becomes visible, we stop and stand motionless, frozen to the spot.

The nun's black habit is unmistakable. It's exactly the dark material worn by Sister Frances, with the black flowing headdress and the band of white to frame her face. But the figure isn't Sister. He towers above us with his huge, broad shoulders, his face fat and flabby with a cushion of double chins. Across his forehead, instead of the locks of Sister's dark brown hair, his scalp is shaved. He reaches his hand out to steady himself as the train rounds the corner, and his forearms are covered in long, black hair. My stomach sinks towards my knees. It's the same man I saw in the automata museum and the man who was standing in the Bonfire Night display. Only this time he's dressed as a nun.

The candlelight dances and twinkles on his flabby face as my hand shakes and trembles. He gazes straight at me as, for the second time today, our eyes meet.

I gasp.

Then I drop the hollowed-out remains of snivelling Sydney on the floor as Marie and I turn round and run.

27

'Just mind that bottle of champagne,' warned Les as the
minibus skidded back on to the main road.

'Don't worry. We've got it safe,' said Ken. ''Ave you
got your eye on that trophy?'

Les nodded, trying not to grin too broadly as he
hugged the John Sanella trophy – a shining silver
Olympic torch – firmly to his chest.

'Let's hope we get there in time.'

None of them could bear to think what might happen
if they didn't reach the train in time. In all their years of
driving, neither Les nor Ken had ever actually seen the
carnage of a train crash. They'd seen photographs of
crashed trains in newspapers and occasionally passed the
wreckage of buckled carriages shunted beside the line.
There were times when Les had had to slam on the
brakes – once when he'd spotted some kids playing on
the line. He'd managed to stop in time, but even the
memory of that awful sense of impending terror still
made his stomach lurch.

Concentrate on the positive, he told himself. Les
steadied the beer crates with his feet as they veered
around another bend, then focused the whole of his
attention on reliving the moment when the Flying Scotsmen had actually won the John Sanella Quiz League
final. Les had had to restrain himself from jumping up
and down with excitement in the golden moment when
he had marched out to the bar to be presented with the
actual – *the actual* – J. Sanella trophy.

'On accepting this trophy, I would like to thank . . .'

He was about to start naming the rest of the team and applauding their individual efforts when, gazing proudly round the room, he became slowly aware of the noticeable lack of enthusiasm on the faces of the Jolly Rogers supporters. Les condensed his speech to an annotated 'Thank you very much' and raised the trophy aloft for only a few brief seconds. They could best celebrate their triumph, he decided, after they'd been escorted out of the pub by the landlord and were smiling away down the road in Carter's hospital minibus.

'Can you check where we are on the map?' Carter asked. 'The road signs are covered up with snow.'

Ken didn't have room to unfold the map, 'Can you pull up?'

Carter shook his head. He was afraid to stop in case the bus wouldn't start again. And he didn't want to waste any more time. He was concentrating the whole of his attention on his driving and on thinking of ways to reassure Donald when he climbed into the cab. He mustn't make Don panic, that was the most important thing. He had to calm him down. He imagined the two of them, Carter with his hand resting gently on Don's massive shoulder. Take it easy, Don. Relax. Everything's O.K.

'The red light's showing on the petrol.'

'It'll be all right. We'll pull up when we get to the village.'

Carter tried to make his own voice sound calm. He tried to sound clear-headed and confident. But the terror of what might happen if they didn't reach the train in time was turning the journey into a nightmare.

You see, Don, he would explain to him, everybody has their nightmares. Some people's nightmares seem tiny and insignificant – like a fear of dogs or a fear of the dark.

Some people though, sadly, have terrible nightmares – things no person should ever have to live with. These are the kind of nightmares that can pick you up and spin you round. They lift you right out of the place where you've always felt safe and they whirl you round in a whirlwind, then stick you down somewhere else – they stick you down on some other tracks a long, long way from home and off you go. Steaming away. Nightmares drive people, Don. Nightmares make you do things you don't really want to do, send you to places you don't really want to go . . .

'Do you want to just look for the petrol can? It's standing next to the snow shovel in the back.'

The way to be happy, Don, is to stop the nightmares driving you. Find ways of getting in control, learn how to steer your own life. And to do that, you have to turn round and meet the nightmares head on, talk about them, write about them, tell people, over and over again. That's the way to make the nightmares lose their grip on you, Don. That's the way to get back in control. The way to drive your own train, build your own tracks, plan your own route.

That's the way to live with a nightmare and survive . . .

★

Marie and I stand huddled together inside the toilet, leaning against the door. The door is locked, but we're not taking any chances. Marie shakes uncontrollably like something left on top of a washing machine. I squeeze my arms around her shoulders and hold her tight.

'He must have done something with Sister,' Marie whimpers. 'Mustn't he? He must have killed her.'

157

I don't know what to say. I do know Sister would be most unlikely to take her clothes off and give them to a strange man on a train.

'He might have strangled her with her crucifix.'

I squeeze Marie tighter.

'He might have thrown her body down on to the rails. We could have run over it.'

I think about the awful juddering and jerking of the train and my stomach turns right over.

'Do you think he'll be . . . looking for us . . .' Marie stares up at me with her eyes open wide '. . . now?'

I turn and glance at the door shut firmly behind us. 'I don't know.'

What I do know is that the train is picking up speed again and our hopes of ever being able to get out and walk seem to be dwindling more and more. 'We'll have to sneak out next time when the train stops.'

Marie nods. 'I know but . . .' she squeezes me tighter, '. . . what if he comes after us?'

I imagine the two of us running along beside the train track pursued by the madman dressed in Sister's habit and waving an axe or . . . I don't actually think we'd get very far, anyway. Neither of us is all that good at running.

'Perhaps we could hide somewhere,' suggests Marie.

I picture us both cowering underneath a hedge beside the track. But then I also see the trail of footprints we'd leave behind us in the snow. The man would see the footprints straightaway and follow them. We wouldn't be able to escape.

There's a squeal of brakes and we're thrown against the window as the train swerves round a bend.

'Do you think there must be two of them?' asks Marie. 'One of them driving the train and one dressed as a nun?'

I shake my head. I don't know. 'Shall I peep outside?'

'No!' Marie grabs hold of my arm and pins it tightly to my side. 'We've got to stay here. At least we're safe in here.'

But as we're tossed and bumped about and, as the tannoy starts to crackle once again, I don't feel as if we're safe at all.

A high-pitched squeaking voice splutters out into the darkness:

The Lord is my shepherd; I shall not want.

'That's what Sister was reading in her Bible.'

'I know.'

I can hear the thumping of Marie's heart, pressed against my own.

'Do you think it might be her?'

I shake my head. 'Sister's voice doesn't shake like that.'

There's a chilling silence. 'You don't think it might be a . . . ghost?'

I feel the hairs stand up again on the back of my neck and right along my arm. I've never heard of a ghost talking down the speaker on a train before:

He maketh me to lie down in green pastures:

the voice goes on:

He leadeth me beside the still waters.

'It'll be the lunatic. He can do everybody's different voices.

He restoreth my soul.

'Perhaps Sister was reading the psalm when . . . when he . . . you know. Perhaps that's how he's learned to do her voice.'

I wish Marie wouldn't talk like that. I'm trying so hard to keep calm and steady and now my legs are shaking and I find it hard to keep standing upright. 'Perhaps,' I whisper, 'we ought to peep outside. I mean, Sister might be . . . she might be tied up somewhere. We ought to have another look.'

Marie clings tightly to my jacket.

I stare at the door.

He leadeth me in the paths of righteousness for his name's
  sake.

It's almost as though, if I stare hard enough, I'll be able to see right through the door and into the corridor beyond.

'Have you still got the matches?'

Marie nods reluctantly. 'Match.'

Just one candle and just one match. I wonder if we ought to save them. It occurs to me that there may be even more dreadful things in store and we might desperately need our only candle and our only match.

Yea, though I walk through the valley of the shadow
  of death . . .

But then I think about walking down the corridor and bumping again into the man dressed as a nun in the pitch darkness and I feel faint and dizzy with fear. If we're going outside again, we'll have to walk down with the lighted candle or not at all.

   . . . I will fear no evil: for thou art with me . . .

Marie produces her candle which has almost melted from her sweating palms. Amazingly, it lights up with our last match.

'I dropped mine.'

'Well, never mind,' says Marie. 'We might find it.'

She holds her candle in the air as I unlock the door. I know there's a Toilet Vacant/Engaged sign illuminated outside in the carriage. If there's anyone waiting for us, they'll know we're opening the door.

I stand and listen.

   . . . thy rod and thy staff they comfort me.

160

When I'm positive I can't hear anything except the rackety-rack of the wheels on the track, I peep outside. I can't see anyone. I open the gap a bit further.

Thou preparest a table before me in the presence of
*   mine enemies:*
thou anointest my head with oil . . .

'Has he gone?'

I nod.

. . . my cup runneth over.

I peer around for the final time before we both step out into the corridor.

Surely goodness and mercy shall follow me all the days of
*   my life:*
and I will dwell in the house of the Lord for ever.

28

'That blasted nun!' yelled Carter, flinging the empty petrol can into the nearest bank of snow.

The others stared in amazement.

'When she couldn't get her car started,' Carter complained, 'she thought she'd run out of petrol. Stupid woman! One of the other nurses offered to fetch her some petrol – they never said it was out of the flippin' Smile-Afrigginway bus.'

The silence drifted between the not-so-Flying Scotsmen like a bank of windswept snow as they considered the awful implications of the fact that they'd now run completely out of petrol.

'Well then,' said Les, 'everybody out.'

Nobody leapt to their feet.

'Come on,' Les urged them. 'Time for another shove.'

After a couple of long, deep sighs, Ken and Orgreave clambered out of the bus with Les whilst Carter made a valiant attempt to restart the engine. It took a husky breath, cleared its throat, coughed, spluttered and died.

''Ave we got them beer crates steady?

'They'll be all right.'

'Let's just see if we can see where we are.'

The blizzard had subsided now and the moonlight gave them a clear view from the crest of the hill, right across the valley. There were sparkling fields and hedges, distant hills humped like coverless cushions and, in the hollow of the valley, rows of tent-like roofs and glistening street lights.

'Well, there's the village,' Ken pointed, 'so that should

be the train line down there.' He traced his finger along the crease of the valley.

Les nodded. 'Got to be.'

They stood and scrutinised the landscape. 'Can't see any sign of a train.'

'Well, that's all right,' said Les. 'It might mean we're in time.'

Both men scoured the seam at the base of the hills for any sign of a locomotive. Everything was still. Ken pointed. 'I think that's where the line goes past that level crossin'.'

Les nodded.

'We can freewheel once we get over the top of the 'ill.'

'Right then,' Les called to Carter. 'We'll just give it a shove. We're not far off the top.'

'OK.'

'You'll be able to let it run all the way down from there. The railway line's at the bottom somewhere.'

Carter peered suspiciously at the road ahead. 'Do you think it looks icy?'

'No, no, you'll be all right,' Les reassured him.

Orgreave and Ken stationed themselves behind the back wheels.

'Right,' ordered Les, ''ave you got that champagne safe?'

'It's fine.'

'Everybody ready?'

Carter released the handbrake. 'OK.'

'Is that trophy all right?'

'It's OK.'

'Right then, 'ere we go!'

★

We creep out into the little space in between the carriages, and gaze along the snaking, interlocking aisles.

'Can you see anything?' Marie whispers.

I check the rows of seats standing stiffly to attention. I check for stray lunatics and nuns. The ranks are reflected in the darkened glass, their numbers doubled and trebled as they rumble and rock away into the distance.

I shake my head.

Of course, the fact that I can't see anyone doesn't mean there's no one there. Marie's candle casts a golden glow along the centre of the carriage, but it can't illuminate the spaces in between the rows of seats. We can't see round the corner into the next space in between the carriages; we can't peer inside the luggage racks and toilets. The fact that we can't see anyone doesn't mean we're safe.

'What shall we do?'

I glance behind us. I think of Sister's Bible, lying on the table next to her briefcase and her coat. I think about going back and fetching it. I imagine myself holding the Bible in my outstretched hand. It would give me something substantial to cling on to as well as demonstrating the irrefutable evidence that Sister has been here, sitting on the train.

But as I gaze along the receding ranks of empty seats, I realise there is no one here to look. No one to care what's happened to Sister Frances. No one except Marie and myself who even knows she's disappeared.

We both stand still and listen. There's only the rackety-rack, rackety-rack of the wheels and the pounding of our hearts.

'Shall we go, then?'

We creep through the next set of doors as they open by themselves and we shuffle along the aisle. We make slow progress because we're walking arm in arm, one behind the other, and we have to keep shielding what's left of our candle from the draught. We haven't found Sydney. He must have rolled away underneath the seats somewhere.

The loudspeaker crackles. I squeeze my hands tightly round Marie's arm as we wait for the announcement. I can hear my heart thumping. I can feel it drumming in my chest as the blood pounds in my brain. 'This is a story about Thomas the Tank Engine,' the speaker tells us.

'Oh.' I give a little gasp.

A story about Thomas and his special friend, Edward the Blue Engine . . .

*

The minibus began to roll more easily as it reached the summit of the hill.

'Right then! Come on, lads!'

Carter was already sitting at the wheel as Orgreave and the Flying Scotsmen flew back inside. Stretching out ahead of him, Carter could see the long, winding road as it spiralled down towards the village.

'Right then! Here we go!'

'Watch out for anybody sledgin',' advised Les.

'Or skiin',' added Ken.

Carter gripped tightly to the wheel as the minibus picked up speed.

'This is all right, eh? We'll be down in no time.'

At the side of the road, abandoned cars were tucked inside the high snow banks. Carter steered skilfully round them.

'Better not be anything comin' the other way,' warned Les. 'There's not a lot o' room.'

The Smile-Away bus rolled faster and faster. Carter steered round a snowdrift then, just to reassure himself, gave a practice tap upon the brake.

Nothing happened.

He gasped.

'What's a matter?' asked Les.

Carter tried to keep calm. 'The brakes.' He pressed his foot full down to the floor. 'The brakes aren't working.'

'That's all right,' Les reassured him. 'It'll be a bit icy, that's all.'

'What . . . what if there's something coming?' Carter couldn't keep the panic from his voice as he slalomed round an abandoned AA recovery vehicle.

'There won't be anything comin' up 'ere,' Les insisted. 'They won't be able to get up the 'ill. Anyway,' he tucked the champagne bottle safely down the gap between the seats, 'we'll soon stop when we get to the bottom.'

Carter skidded round a sharp bend in the road. 'We're going faster.'

'You'll be all right.' Les pressed the John Sanella Trophy tightly against his chest, 'you've passed your drivin' test, haven't you?'

'I think that was a thirty-miles-an-hour sign,' observed Orgreave.

'Do you think I ought to try the handbrake?'

'No!' Les almost screamed. 'Not at this speed. We'll tip right over.'

The minibus rolled into the outskirts of the village, past the church and then the butcher's. Ken was about to make a joke about the undertaker's as they flew towards the funeral parlour but then thought better of it. He held on to the door as they sped through a red traffic light and straight across a junction.

'Have you got that beer steady?' asked Les.

'It's all right,' said Ken. 'I've got my foot on it.'

'We're going faster.' Carter's voice was slightly hysterical as they rattled the wrong way along a one-way street then slipped and skidded round a small traffic island.

'Oh dear,' said Orgreave. 'I'm feeling a bit sick.'

'Keep your mouth shut, then,' said Les.

'Close your eyes,' said Ken.

Orgreave screwed his eyes up tight and clung hold of the front seat. 'What if there's a train comin' at the bottom?'

'Don't worry,' Les told him. 'If there is, the gates'll go down at the level crossing.'

'I know but, how will we . . . ?'

Everyone held their breath as the minibus pulled out to overtake an abandoned lorry, parked in the middle of the High Street.

'That was a bit close,' said Ken as they scraped the lorry's wing mirror.

'You're doin' all right, Carter,' said Les. 'Don't take any notice. Just keep steerin'.'

Carter kept testing his foot on the brake but still there was no response.

'Leave the brake alone,' advised Les. 'It'll only make us skid.'

'Are we there yet?' asked Orgreave.

'Shut up an' go back to sleep.'

Even Carter closed his eyes as he failed to negotiate a roundabout. The minibus swerved and skidded and leant over on two wheels. Carter wrenched the steering wheel round with an awesome screech.

'What's that funny noise?' asked Orgreave.

'It's us,' said Ken.

Carter got the bus back on all four wheels but facing straight towards the central island.

'Hope there's nothing coming.'

Undeterred, he rattled the bus straight up the kerb and across the snow-covered grass.

'Hope they didn't have no crocuses comin' up,' said Ken.

They tripped down the kerb at the other side and passed a sign for a humpbacked bridge.

'At least there's not much traffic about,' observed Les.

'Perhaps they've seen us comin'.'

The roundabout had slowed the minibus down. It lost even more of its momentum as it approached the river.

'Just keep going across that bridge,' Les advised. 'Don't go into the water.'

Carter opened his mouth to swear at Les but decided to save his breath.

'We're doin' all right,' said Ken. 'Nearly there.'

'Level crossing coming up,' announced Les.

'Better not be a train.'

The barriers were up as the minibus approached. But by now the road had levelled out and they were slowing to a crawl.

'Keep going,' Les advised. 'You don't want to stop in the middle of the train lines.'

Carter took a deep breath. 'I can't help where we stop,' he almost screamed. 'It's not my fault, is it?'

The Smile-Away bus hit a bank of snow beside the train lines; it jolted, slowed down, then almost stopped.

'Come on. Keep going.'

'Come on!'

'Come on!'

'Come on!' Carter shouted. He had one final attempt at engaging the gears and the bus stuttered forward.

'Hooray! We're off again!'

But their excitement was short-lived. The bus staggered across the first set of lines.

'There's not a train comin', is there?'

'Hurry up!'

But then the Smile-Away bus began to smile no longer. Overcome with exhaustion, its front wheels rested on the second train line before it decided it could go no further. The bus spluttered once more, stopped and finally ground to a halt right in the middle of the train track.

29

Edward is always kind to big engines . . .

I listen in astonishment as the squeaky, high-pitched voice tells us all about Edward the kind engine who looks after small engines when they get into difficulties. It's the story of Thomas and his special friend, Edward, that I bought to take home to the twins. The story that went missing from my bag. Normally, it's very comforting to hear stories about the make-believe world where trains have smiling faces and care about each other.

. . . he's kind to all the engines, even if they're rude or impatient.

But hearing the story read in a runaway train that seems about to crash, only serves to remind me of how far we are from normality. It reminds me that I should have walked several hours ago into our house with my carrier bag and given the twins and Lianne their presents.

Now we should be sitting comfortably by the fireside while I read them their story about Edward, the nice kind train with the smiling face. I would have pointed out the illustrations in the book, all the cute little engines with their bright, happy faces, who have different, interesting personalities and who talk just like real people. I'd have shown them the picture of the Fat Controller who's in charge of everything, who's reliable and sensible even though he does get cross.

The train shrieks around a bend as Marie and I are battered against a table.

'Oh no! What's he doing now?'

'Are you hurt?'

'No. No, I'm all right.' I've actually jolted my back but I don't say so. I stand up straight and take a few deep breaths as Marie deposits her splodge of melted candle on the table. 'The candle's gone out.'

We haven't any more matches.

If the other engines misbehave, Edward calms everyone down.

We could do with Edward here at the moment, calming *us* down, telling us everything will be all right, restoring order in a world of anarchy and chaos. But the fairy-tale world of Edward and Thomas the Tank Engine is a long, long way away.

I give Marie a little nudge and gesture towards the next carriage because what we have to do now, of course, is walk down into the guard's van and then make our way through to the driver.

I squeeze my hand tightly around the top of Marie's arm. We have to go down and look inside the guard's van and the driver's cab because we think that Sister Frances might be lying there unconscious or tied up. That's if she's still alive. But walking through the guard's van and into the driver's cab seems like the longest journey in the world as we both become more and more certain that this train is being driven by a lunatic.

In front of us is the door. There isn't far to go. I stand and wait for a moment because I'm feeling shaky. When people feel scared, they talk about having butterflies. That means that the shaking they feel is like the fluttering of a butterfly's wings inside their tummy. But the shaking I feel is more like a flock of pigeons, all of them fluttering at once. My hands are trembling and my throat is parched.

We inch our way forward towards the door.

*

'Ohhh dear.'

'What a place to stop!'

'Oh dear! Oh dear! Oh dear!'

'This doesn't look too good.'

There was a frozen silence as Orgreave and the grounded Flying Scotsmen glanced anxiously along the track. The polished parallel rails gleamed sharply in the moonlight. There was no sign of a train.

'Come on then, lads,' announced Les. 'Everybody out.'

Carter left the keys in the lock so they could steer the bus clear. He opened his door and climbed out, then plodded round the back of the bus, clearing a space with his sleeves all ready to push. 'Right then! Are we ready?'

Then Carter realised he was standing in the middle of the train tracks all by himself. 'What's a matter? Where've you all gone?'

But the other Flying Scotsmen had a completely different set of priorities. 'Right,' ordered Les, 'if Ken an' Orgreave take that first crate . . .' he helped to manoeuvre it through the door, 'then Carter an' me can take this one.'

'What the . . . ?' Carter was horrified. 'What on earth do you think you're doing? There could be a train any minute.'

'I know,' said Les, lifting the first crate out of the way. 'That's why we're rescuin' the beer.'

Carter swallowed his swear words and took a long deep breath as he tried single-handedly to push the minibus clear of the lines. It refused to budge. 'Hurry up!'

'Won't be long. Just give us an 'and with this other crate.'

172

'You're mad!' Carter checked into the distance for any sign of approaching lights . . .

'You won't say that when you're drinkin' the beer.'

. . . before reluctantly leaving the bus in order to carry the second crate to safety.

'Are you sure that's not a train?' asked Orgreave.

Carter, stopped with his beer crate in midair and gazed along the track. 'I can't see anything.'

'I'll just get the champagne,' offered Ken.

But Orgreave was aware of a low rumbling in the distance. 'I'm sure I can hear a noise.'

'Well, I can't see anything,' said Carter.

They bedded down the crates in a pile of snow at the edge of the track. 'Right,' said Les, 'that'll keep 'em nice an' cool. Now let's get this bus moved.'

'Orgreave thinks he can hear a train,' said Carter.

'You can see the lights from a long way off,' Les explained. 'We'll soon see one if it comes.'

*

Marie and I creep inside the guard's van. There aren't any seats, just a kind of wire cage. Of course, we can't see it properly because we no longer have any light. The guard's van is darker than the rest of the train. It doesn't have any windows.

Marie and I still cling tightly to each other. My head feels light and empty as though I'm going to faint and I still have the sick, dry feeling in my throat. Both of us are shaking but we don't intend to turn back now. We have to find out what's happened to Sister Frances.

'And what do you think Edward the Blue Engine did next?' a voice asks over the speaker.

I don't care any more. I don't care about Edward the Blue Engine. And I'm tired of trying to work out who's saying what and who they're talking to. I'm tired of trying to work out which is the driver and which is the lunatic and just how many lunatics there are. I creep forward with Marie.

What I keep telling myself is that before much longer, this will all be over. It can't go on forever. Every nightmare comes to an end. And, if we do survive, then all this will just be a story that we tell people afterwards: 'Just listen about what happened on our day out to York . . .' we'll say. If we don't survive, we won't be able to tell the story but we probably won't know anything about it either.

We stumble forward with our hands stretched out in front of us.

Marie stops. 'There's the door.'

There's only one door at the end of the guard's van and it doesn't open by itself. Nor does it have a window for us to peep through. It's a heavy steel door with a big handle, the sort you'd expect to find in a factory or a warehouse. It's as if all the modern gadgets and the fancy furnishings have turned back into pumpkins at the front end of the train. We're leaving behind the fairy-tale land of nice tables and comfy seats alongside the make-believe world where engines talk nicely to each other and all have smiling faces.

I rest my hand on the cold steel handle and take a deep breath.

First of all, I listen but I can only hear the clackety-clack of the wheels rumbling over the rails. I can't hear any voices.

'Shall we go in?' Marie whispers.

I don't feel like going in. I feel more like turning round and running back as fast as my legs will carry me. I feel more like bursting into tears.

But I don't.

I unfasten the door. It isn't easy to open because the door is very heavy. However, I give the door a push and peep inside.

It takes several seconds before our eyes adjust. The cab is lighter than the guard's van because there are big windows in the front, and the white snow is reflecting the moonlight. Because it all seems so much brighter, it takes us a while to get accustomed to the light.

However, it doesn't take us long to focus on the people sitting inside the cab. There's a nun and a train driver. The nun is driving the train and the train driver is sitting on a stool reading what looks suspiciously like one of my Thomas the Tank Engine books. The nun, however, isn't Sister Frances. The nun is the man we saw earlier – the big man from the Guy Fawkes display – only he's still wearing Sister's habit and her head-dress.

Sitting beside him with my book is Sister Frances, only she's wearing the train driver's uniform and cap. The scene is so amazing that both Marie and myself just stand and stare. We find it hard to believe our eyes.

The nun and the train driver don't turn round. That isn't because they haven't heard us opening the door. The reason they don't turn round is because their eyes are fixed on the scene in front. I look ahead to where they're both staring and then I gasp out loud.

A long way in front of us is a vehicle parked right in the middle of the train lines. It's a kind of large white van, a bit like an ice-cream van. There are other lights flashing as well, red and orange. I don't know what the lights are for but I can see them reflecting on the snow. The driver of the train – the person dressed as a nun – has seen the van and is starting to apply the brakes.

However, the train is travelling very, very fast. I don't really see how we can stop in time.

*

Ken settled the bottle of champagne together with the crates of beer. Then the four of them ran back and stood behind the bus. 'Right,' said Les. 'Everybody ready?'

Orgreave glanced apprehensively along the lines. 'I think it's gettin' nearer.'

'Just close your ears, Orgreave,' Les advised. 'Now we've just got to lift it over this rail.'

The bus had stopped in an awkward position with its front wheels stuck on the train lines. 'One big shove,' said Les. 'Right!'

They all put their weight behind it but the bus wouldn't move. 'Right, try again. One more time.'

By now, there was a definite humming through the train lines. The bus inched forwards.

'Come on,' ordered Les, 'put some weight behind it.'

They all shoved again and the bus began to roll. As Ken placed his foot on the train line, however, he felt a definite vibration. 'Do you know,' he said, 'that does sound like a train.'

Everyone stopped and listened. By now, the humming was unmistakeable. 'But there's no lights,' argued Les. 'There's no trains run without lights.'

'We'd better make a move!' shouted Carter.

The rumbling grew louder and louder. 'Which way's it comin'?'

'I don't know, but we'd better stand back!' yelled Ken.

'Get out of the way!' panicked Orgreave.

They rushed to the side of the lines for safety but,

just at that moment, Les remembered the John Sanella trophy. 'Hey up!' he yelled. 'Who's got the trophy?'

Everyone looked around. No one had picked it up.

'It was on the back seat,' said Carter.

'You fool. What d'you leave it there for?'

'You're never goin' back for it!'

But Les was already leaping back across the train lines.

'Les!'

'Don't be daft, Les,' shouted Orgreave. 'Just leave it!'

'Leave it!' yelled Carter.

'Leave it!' yelled Ken.

By now, the barriers at the side of the road were being lowered. Red lights flashed from the level crossing, shining across the snow.

'Les! Don't be a fool!' yelled Orgreave.

Bells were ringing at the side of the track.

Les dived into the minibus. He groped around for the trophy.

'Les!'

His hands rested on the cold steel of the Olympic torch.

'Les!'

He lifted up the trophy and clambered out of the bus.

And, at that minute, the delayed 16.50 train from York came tearing along the track. Les stood, frozen with astonishment to see the train tearing towards him at full speed.

'Les!'

'Les!'

He realised that the locomotive was being driven without any lights. He realised that, if we was going to survive, he needed to leap out of the way faster than he'd ever leapt before.

'Les!'

But also, in the split second before the message was relayed down to his legs, he managed to see the figure sitting in the cab.

'Les!'

As Les stood poised with his silver trophy held aloft, he became aware of a figure whose face was framed by a band of white. A band of white and a black headdress.

'Les!'

As the locomotive came tearing down the track towards him, Les became suddenly aware that his train was being driven by a nun.

*

I only have time to stare at the scene for a second before Marie and I start falling forward. Throughout our nightmare train ride, we've got used to the train braking suddenly and throwing us about but it's as though the driver's just been practising for this. He tenses his body. His mouth opens in a silent scream. The muscles stand out on his hairy arms as if his sinews are made of steel.

I try to steady myself but it's no good. I start to topple into the arms of Sister Frances. As I fall, I catch a glimpse of a figure standing in the middle of the train lines. He's standing in front of the white van and he's holding something in the air. I think he's waving. He seems to be waving a giant ice-cream cornet. Of course, I can't understand what's going on. It's a ridiculous place for anyone to park their ice-cream van and a really stupid time of night for anyone to be buying an ice cream.

178

When I was a little girl in the infants school, our teacher told us a silly rhyme that went: *I scream; you scream; we all scream for ice cream.*

And that's just what we do. All of us. I scream and Marie screams and the nun and the train driver scream as well. I don't know what the man with the ice-cream cornet does because I just can't see him any more. The door slams shut behind us. Marie and I are thrown forward. We bang our bodies against the seats. Everything spins around. There are stars and ice-cream cornets flashing in my head. My eardrums squirm with the squealing of the brakes and the terrible screams of terror. Then we all slide to the floor, clinging to each other, still screaming, waiting for the crash.

30

'It all happened when I was very small,' Don explains to Sister Frances as they sit by the window together, sharing a bag of chips. 'Only a little lad.' He pauses for a moment with a piece of fishcake halfway to his mouth. 'I don't suppose you've ever had any children at all . . . have you . . . ?'

Sister lays down her chips for a moment, crosses her palms then gazes piously out of the window. 'Some things,' she answers cryptically, 'are best left unexplained: secrets between ourselves and God.' She pops a piece of battered sausage into her mouth. 'And anyway, I'm . . . I'm a bride of Christ.'

'Oh, I see.'

Marie and I exchange glances but say nothing. Our mouths are full of steaming, hot, salty, vinegar-coated chips.

'Anyway,' Don explains, 'there was this accident. It was on Bonfire Night. My dad – Loxley – he was driving the train.' He pauses and shakes his head, a faraway look in his eye. 'There were bodies, bodies everywhere, bits of limbs – bits of arms and legs . . .'

I stop chewing for a moment.

'There were lots of people killed.'

Carter – the man who's Donald's nurse – reaches across and rests his hand gently on Don's shoulder. 'So you see,' he says, 'what Dr Pattram said was true. You've had this obsession, Don, not with trains, but with train crashes. Ever since that awful day, you've been trying to relive the trauma, trying to . . . well, trying to make things crash.'

Don takes a large bite of his fishcake. 'No, no, that's not right.' He shakes his massive head. 'No, I haven't been trying to *make* things crash. You see, when I was in the cab that day, I was fastened in a kind of safety harness, something my dad had made for me – probably saved my life. But, when my dad had his heart attack, I knew I had to try and stop that train. I could see this other train – the one that had broken down – in the distance. Although I was only very small, I knew how to drive a train and I knew how to stop one as well. All I needed to do was just put my foot down on the brake. Of course,' he shakes his head, 'I couldn't reach it. I was much too small, you see, and I was all fastened up.'

There's a sympathetic silence. I go back to eating my chips.

'When I stopped the train just now – when I put the brakes on, when I stopped us crashing – that's the kind of thing I've been dreaming about ever since. That's something I've been wanting to do ever since the accident.'

'Well, you certainly saved everybody's life,' says Carter.

'I didn't realize, of course, that anybody's life had been saved until quite a long time after we'd stopped. Right at the very last minute, I must have just passed out. When I eventually opened my eyes, I thought there'd been a crash and I'd missed it. I even wondered if everyone had died. When I saw the flashing red lights and heard the strange bells ringing, I even began to wonder if I was on my way to heaven.

'All I ever wanted was to have my time over again, to find a way of going back and pressing my foot down on that pedal. All I wanted was to erase the sight of all those bodies scattered around the embankment. All I wanted was to be a hero – the one that saved every-body's life.'

I remember the distant figure, pausing, staring, as if he were hypnotised, as the train approached at break-neck speed. I remember wondering why he was buying such a large ice cream in such cold weather in such a strange place at such a funny time of night. And I re-member thinking, as I toppled to the floor, how upset my mum would be when she found out that I was dead. I thought about how she'd have to explain the news to Lianne and to the twins. I thought she might see the crash on the evening news on TV.

Of course, what I didn't see was the man with the big cornet running for cover. In the same way that some-times, in a car, you think you must have run over a pigeon in the street because you haven't actually seen it fly away. The reason you haven't seen it is because it hasn't flown away until the very last second. That's what happened to Les, the man standing by the van. 'I didn't know I'd even got away,' he told us. 'Not until I was lying face down in the snow.'

'What Teresa and I found hard to understand though, Sister,' explains Marie, tucking into her bat-tered cod and mushy peas, 'is why you changed clothes with Don. I mean, when we saw him wearing your habit – well, we just thought something awful must have happened.'

Sister nods. 'Well, girls, you see, I was extremely worried about Donald's ability to drive a train. When I realised that the train was being driven so inexpertly, I marched straight down to the cab and suggested taking over. Of course, he insisted that only someone wearing a train driver's uniform was allowed to drive a train so that meant changing clothes.'

182

Marie and I gaze at each other in total incredulity. The idea that Sister would think she can drive even a shopping trolley better than anyone else is too ridiculous for words.

'A lesson to us all, girls,' Sister goes on, 'to always wear several layers of . . .' she pauses '. . . respectable undergarments, ready for any emergency.'

Of course, Marie and I could never imagine Sister wearing any clothing that isn't totally respectable. Although we've often speculated on what nuns wear underneath their habits, our imagination has usually centred on long thermal underwear, crepe stockings and knickers that reach to their knees.

Don takes another bottle out of the half-empty crate resting on the table. 'I know you'll find this hard to believe,' he explains, 'but it turned out that she was an even worse driver than I am.'

Marie and I discreetly wipe the chuckles from our faces. We long ago came to the conclusion that the driving examiner let Sister pass her test only because he was terrified of ever having to sit beside her in a car again. 'We know exactly what you mean,' Marie mutters.

Just in case you're wondering, we're all sitting round two tables, eating the very best fish 'n' chip supper I have ever tasted; the conductor, whose name turns out to be Orgreave – not Peter Penguin – managed to persuade the driver to stop at the nearest fish 'n' chip shop.

So now we've phoned our parents and told them we're all right; the snow has stopped and we're being driven back home by a sensible train driver called Les. Outside, we can see the buildings on the outsksirts of Sheffield, the glistening dome of Meadowhall still covered in its Christmas fairy-lights, the silver moonlight sparkling on the River Don. The world outside is like a picture in a fairy story. A fairy tale where even the most terrifying nightmares have a happy ending. When trains stop in the very nick of time just before they crash, where dangerous lunatics turn out to be quite nice people really, where ordinary people win the best prizes and we all live happily ever after.

'You see,' Don explains to Carter as he finishes his fishcake, 'I'm very grateful for all your help and everything, but, well – I just think I ought to explain that – you see, I never really thought I was a train.'

There's a pause. Of course, Marie and I don't understand what he's on about. We just concentrate on enjoying the rest of our chips.

'It's just that, when they sent me to St Aiden's,' Don continues, 'it seemed appropriate somehow. The place had that sort of an effect on me. Actually,' he adds a little sheepishly, 'I'm all right now.'

We all nod sympathetically.

'Well,' says Sister, 'I must confess that I think it's hardly the best place for someone to go to try and sort out their problems. It would certainly have sent me right off the rails.'

'It'd have given you the wrong train of thought,' adds Orgreave.

'Put you on quite the wrong tracks,' contributes Ken.

'It would have made it very hard for you to express yourself,' explains Carter.

Don nods. 'Well, all the signals were that I was running out of steam, and that place was the end of the line.' He wipes his remaining chips round the puddle of vinegar settled in the centre of the greaseproof paper. 'So,' he says. He pauses and thinks for a moment and then looks up at Sister Frances, 'If I'm not really a train . . . are you really a bride of Christ . . . or what?'

We all turn to Sister, expectantly. I nudge Marie. Marie nudges me. There's a long pause.

Sister opens her mouth and closes it, she raises a chip to her lips, then she puts it down. For only the second time since I've known her, Sister Frances seems completely lost for words.

When it seems to be the end of that conversation, Carter turns back to Don: 'One thing I'm still curious about, though, Don,' Carter asks, 'is, if you really didn't want to make things crash – if all you wanted was to rescue everybody – why did you never manage to prevent a crash when Myrtle Springs was around? I mean, you didn't manage to stop the wheelie bin tipping rubbish all over her car, did you?'

Don screws up his empty chip wrapper. He thinks for a moment, then gives Carter a sly grin. 'Some things,' he tells him, imitating Sister's high-pitched voice, 'some things are perhaps best left unexplained – secrets between ourselves and God.'

31

Marie and I sit behind Sister Frances in front of the large silver crucifix in the centre of the stage. Sister stares up and down the rows of palpitating pupils, giving them all The Stare, refusing to speak until everyone is silent, until the sound of every last shuffle has died away and until everyone's eyes are fixed upon her face.

'So, you've all heard the story about Marie and Teresa and their nightmare journey,' she announces in slow, measured tones. 'The question now for us to ask is . . . who was responsible?'

Years seven and eight are sitting in the first few rows, their minds still stunned by the story of our amazing exploits.

On the table in front of Sister stands the Nightmare Express game that Marie and I have constructed, inspired by one of the models in the automata museum. It's made out of cardboard tubes, bits of string, empty liquorice allsorts cartons and a Thomas the Tank Engine plastic train.

'Remember everyone that one small slip, just one small slip is all it takes to lead us down the slippery slope.'

At this point, to our great dismay, Sister drops a silver ball-bearing down the helter-skelter slide. We've already attempted to explain that the model is only there to be looked at. We haven't actually made it strong enough to operate just yet.

'I am well aware . . .' Sister scrutinises the collective consciences around the hall '. . . there will be those in this room who've forgotten to do their homework; those who drop litter in the school corridor . . .' Sister goes on to explain how these small slips are the first steps along the pathway for lost souls, leading to the high-security unit in St Aiden's Psychiatric Hospital.

'If we take the story right back to its beginnings,' she drops another silver ball-bearing down the chute, 'you might consider that a certain travelling salesman from Wath-on-Dearne might have had a part to play. A man . . .' Sister laces her words here with suitable contempt '. . . who seduced another man's wife.'

The rows of pupils gaze in fascination as the silver ball begins to slide along our arrangement of see-through tunnels and tiny tracks.

'You might consider that Loxley's wife Rivelin, who ran off with another man, leaving her husband to look after their small child, also bears a certain responsibility.' Another ball-bearing . . .

And so the story goes on. I reach out to clasp Marie's hand behind the backs of our seats. Both of us have our fingers crossed. The silver balls land on one of the two liquorice allsort box-lids which form a rather shaky set of scales. When the weight of the pan reaches a certain level it should drop down, seesawing its partner into the air. This pan contains the plastic Thomas the Tank Engine which is on temporary loan from the twins.

'And what about the staff in the hospital?' Sister asks. 'Did the psychiatrists really find out as much as possible about Don's past?'

When the train rises high enough, it should draw level with the gate to another chute and then begin its downhill slide.

'Did they do everything possible to help Donald get better and lead a normal life?' I've a feeling that Sister

Frances has very little time for the people in charge of St Aiden's. That's hinted at by the number of ball bearings she flings down the chute in quick succession.

Marie looks down towards the floor, shaking her head. We were supposed to be having our pictures taken with the model for the local newspaper this afternoon. The way things are going, by the time the photographer arrives, there'll be little more than a pile of squashed cardboard for us both to pose alongside.

'And of course, we have to consider the men who were responsible for looking after the train . . .' Another two ball-bearings roll down the chute. 'Les Carr and his young conductor, Orgreave.'

Although Marie and myself worked out the names of all the different characters involved, we didn't actually give them any points. The idea is that the people who play the game have to decide who was responsible. Of course, we came up with the idea after the amazing success of our Margaret Clitherow game which has just been on display in the school foyer.

The final ball spins down the slide, the scales begin to tip, the train is raised in the air and the gates are opened. The idea is that all this should take place slowly – one ball bearing every few minutes as people turn over their cards. Sister, however, has walloped so many balls on the scales at once that the train shoots into the air, leaps on to the slide and whizzes round and round the helter-skelter.

'Just think about this young man, hungry and cold, what harm would it do, he thought, just to take those few small steps to the fish and chip shop? But those steps were the very last straw – the last straw that caused the train to be driven off its normal . . .'

It's at this point that the train should land on the level crossing at the bottom. Unfortunately, it's gathered so much momentum that it whizzes straight off the rails and skims through the air. Sister reaches out to catch it but her hands just clap together in the empty air. The little smiling engine flies right off the stage, across the seated rows, straight towards Bernadette Dronfield. Bernadette ducks but, as she leans over, her weight causes the whole line of pupils to tip over like a row of knocked-down dominoes.

'Remember children, that it's never too late to get back on your feet,' explains Sister, trying to ignore the fact that quite a large section of the school is now lying horizontally on the floor.

'Remember,' she instructs everyone, as Marie and I struggle to iron the creases from our faces, 'that we must always stay on the right tracks. And now this morning's hymn . . .'

Sister walks across the stage and seats herself at the shining, black, grand piano, a gift to the school from the parents of one of Agnes's tragic victims. Ms Maltby, who's recently joined our school after her successful teaching practice, picks up her electric guitar. Sister Frances readjusts her habit and places her music on the stand.

Now you might imagine that nuns would play the piano gently and sedately. You might imagine that, in a Catholic school, we'd have classical music, Gregorian chants and old-fashioned hymns.

But you'd be wrong.

Ms Maltby plugs in her electric guitar, strides towards the piano and motions us to stand. Suddenly there's an explosion of sound. Sister Frances pounds a boogie-woogie bass. Ms Maltby wails her guitar like an ambulance in a traffic jam as we all start to chorus:

189

I'm on the right track with Jesus
I'm on the right line with the Lord –
He will take me by the hand
And lead me to the promised land –
Oh yes, I'm on the right track with the Lord.

Ms Maltby raises her right knee, bringing her guitar up to her chest, then hops across the stage in time to the music like an ageing rock star. At this point, Sister slips off her shoes and pounds the pedals with her black, wrinkled, woolly socks.

Oh yes, I'm on the right track with Je-e-sus
I'm on the right lines with the Lo-o-rd.
When I wake up each day
I get down on my knees and pray
Oh yes, I'm on the right track with the Lord.

Ms Maltby lays down her guitar for a moment and steps towards years seven and eight clapping her hands in time to Sister Frances's honky-tonk syncopation.

Marie and I exchange glances as the juniors take up the beat, clapping with enthusiasm.

Ms Maltby sidesteps up and down the aisle, clapping her hands in exaggerated movements as if she's squeezing a balloon.

Bernadette copies her, spreading her arms so widely she starts to knock the whole of her row flying towards the floor again:

I'm on the right track with Jesus
I'm on the right lines with the Lord –
He will take me by the hand
And lead me to the promised land –
Oh yes, I'm on the right track with the L-o-o-o-rd.